The Bantam Menace

A Small Town Murder Mystery

Kirsten Weiss

misterio press

Copyright

About the Book

BREAK IN WEDDING SHOES ✓
Walk through venue ✓
Solve murder.

Reformed control-freak Susan has organized the perfect rustic mountain wedding with the love of her life, Arsen Holiday. But when an early arriving guest is found dead, Susan doesn't have a contingency plan for murder.

Susan will have to tread carefully to avoid provoking her soon-to-be in-laws as she unravels the mysteries in Arsen's past. And she'll have to move faster than a bridesmaid leaping for the bouquet. Because a cunning killer seems determined to stop the wedding. At any cost.

If you love quirky heroines, twisty mysteries, and laugh-out-loud humor, you'll love *The Bantam Menace*, book eight in the Wits' End cozy mystery novels. Buy *The Bantam Menace* and start this hilarious caper today!

Contents

Chapter 1

"I SAID," ARSEN'S AUNT Anabelle trilled, "there's been a *murder*."

I laughed weakly. "Excellent. Who's been killed?"

We'd played a murder mystery game last weekend and had laughed until we'd cried. But with one week before the wedding, I was on a strict schedule. Time for more mystery games wasn't on it.

"The... sofa," she said, indistinct. Static crackled in my ear. Frowning, I swiped the butcher block counter with a yellow sponge. Phone reception can be spotty in Doyle. I'd tried three different phone services, and none were reliable.

"A furniture murder? That is a tragedy." I gazed out the open window above the kitchen sink. Behind the roses, a crow hopped along the picket fence. Summer clouds floated above the western mountains.

So what if my eyes burned because the neighbor's new rooster had been up before the dawn? The B&B's kitchen smelled like bacon and coffeecake, and that was always a bonus.

Even better, in one short week, I would be marrying the perfect man. It put minor inconveniences in perspective, and warmth bubbled in my heart.

Her voice crackled. "—veil."

My insides spasmed. "What?" I dropped the sponge on the counter. "Couldn't your friend restore the wedding veil?"

Next Saturday I'd be wearing the vintage wedding gown that had belonged to Arsen's mother. Luckily for me, his aunts had kept his mother's wedding dress in storage. It was gorgeous and had fit me near perfectly. But the veil had yellowed. And I'd really thought it was fixable.

Arsen didn't remember much about his parents. They'd died in a car accident when he was young. He'd been raised by his aunts Judith and Anabelle.

Considering how he'd turned out, I owed them. Big time.

I swallowed. "That's all right," I said. "I have an alternate." The loss of the veil was disappointing, but I had two other veils in reserve. Because she who fails to plan, plans to have at *least* one wedding disaster.

"An alternative for what?" Anabelle asked.

"The veil," I said patiently.

"Why are you talking about the veil? The veil's coming along fine. But there's been a *murder*. Honestly, Susan, I thought you'd take this better. You *love* murders."

My heart beat faster. Obviously we were still talking about the mystery game, because *no one* loves murders. True, I'd solved several. Also true, the sheriff relied on my expertise. And I did get satisfaction from both. But love? *Hardly.*

"What *exactly* has been murdered?" I asked, smothering my frustration. It was the twenty-first century. Why couldn't someone improve mountain cell phone reception?

"Not what. *Who*. Or is it whom? Never mind. The police are here, and so is Arsen. He's terribly upset. It was his old *au pair*, you see. She's dead. Murdered. Really murdered, and—"

Sophie Gagnon? "I'll be right there." I disconnected, grabbed my purse off the table and raced for the kitchen door, my stomach hardening. A *murder? Arsen's old au pair?*

Bailey yipped from his dog bed. I pivoted and grabbed my planners off the kitchen table. "Dixie will be here any minute," I told the beagle. "I'm not sure when I'll be back."

Which just goes to show how rattled I was. It wasn't the sort of detailed communication Bailey would understand. I checked my watch. *Ten AM.*

I raced through the swinging door and across the foyer's faux-Persian carpet. My last paying guests before the wedding made their way down the green-carpeted stairs with their suitcases.

"Oh, hi, Susan," the husband, a pleasant fifty-something said. "Do we need to sign anything to check out?"

I walked backward toward the front door. "Just leave the key cards on the desk. I'm sorry, there's been an emergency, and I have to leave. I hope you had a wonderful stay." I raced onto the Victorian's porch, down the steps and to my Crosstrek.

Watching for neighbor kids, I backed from the gravel drive. School would have started by this hour. But it was late enough for the younger children to begin appearing with balls and tricycles. The court was empty, however, as I turned the small SUV.

Had I heard wrong? Was this all a terrible dream? I glanced at Wits' End. Sunlight glinted off the UFO in its mansard roof. My departing guests peered curiously through the porch's screened door.

A *murder.* My knuckles whitened on the steering wheel. Okay, I *hadn't* planned for that contingency.

I glanced at the planners on the seat beside me. One was strictly for the wedding. The other was for life, and it contained a section specifically for murder investigations. I might not have a plan, but I did have standard operating procedures. And Arsen and I would figure this out together.

Forcing myself to keep to the speed limit, I drove up the pine-clad mountain. Arsen's aunts lived in a mansion with a view of the Sierra lakes below. And no, I was not exaggerating when I described the place as a mansion. Not even a little. Arsen's family was loaded.

I drove through the iron gates. At some point, the front lawn had been turned into a nine-hole golf course for Judith.

The aunts had recently updated the mansion, built in the fifties. But they'd kept the bones—the sloping roofs, the walls of windows, the stone base and wooden second stories. It was spectacular, but I was glad I didn't live in it. Imagine the dusting.

Lights from law enforcement SUVs reflected in the home's ginormous windows. A uniformed deputy walked toward my slowing car. He motioned for me to stop. I braked and rolled down my window.

Deputy Connor Hernandez leaned in. He adjusted the broad-brimmed hat on his curly, dark hair and grimaced. "Hey, Susan. This isn't a good time."

"Anabelle called me."

He straightened and sighed. "All right. I guess you can go in."

"Thank you." *Ha.* Of *course* I could go in. Not only was I the sheriff's best friend, this house belonged to my family. Or at least they'd be my family soon.

The driveway was packed with emergency vehicles. I turned off the ignition, jammed my planners in my oversized purse, and jogged toward the house. A deputy at the door eyed me but didn't say anything as I hurried past.

The foyer was empty. It felt even emptier because it was so big, with stylized marble flooring. Wide floating stairs with modern metal railings led up to the second floor. A tiled walkway that looked like running water led toward the back rooms.

I glanced into the massive living rooms on the left and the right. They were spacious and silent.

Striding down the tile walkway, I moved to the back of the house. I am also not exaggerating when I say it took me several minutes and one wrong turn to get there.

Tall windows overlooked a rectangular swimming pool. Beyond it lay a pond dotted with granite boulders. A landscape of granite and pines and shimmering lakes sprawled in the distance.

On the patio, Arsen towered over his two aunts. His muscular arms cradled their shoulders. They watched sheriff's deputies bustle about on the lawn below.

I slid open a glass door. The three turned at the sound. And though the Sierra air was the same as at Wits' End, here it felt more rarefied.

Judith frowned at her sister. "You called Susan?" She gave her head a shake. The close-cropped, iron-gray hair didn't budge. Judith's face was angular. Her sporty, short-sleeved blouse revealed the sinewy muscles in her arms.

"Of course I did." Anabelle, rounder and softer, her longish gray hair in a ponytail, hurried to me. We hugged. Her loose pink top didn't match her cheerful yellow slacks. But the ensemble looked comfortable.

"One of Susan's wedding guests was murdered," Anabelle continued. "She had to know. And poor Arsen." She stepped away from me and sniffed.

I took Arsen's hand. "I'm so sorry."

Pain creased his handsome face, tanned and square-jawed. He ran his other hand through his whiskey-colored hair. "I'm fine." He wore a golf shirt with his security company logo on the breast. The outfit was as inoffensive as a salesman's. But Arsen couldn't help looking dangerous and masculine.

"What happened?" I asked.

Judith folded her arms. "I went for my after-breakfast walk at nine AM. After looping the golf course, I walked along the lakeview path. I found Sophie at exactly nine-twenty-three. She appeared to have been bludgeoned. She was dead."

I pulled out my regular planner and made notes. Judith made an admirable witness—direct and to the point. "Bludgeoned with what?"

"No idea," Judith said. "There were no obvious weapons nearby."

"This explains why we didn't see Sophie at breakfast this morning," Anabelle said breathlessly.

"I called the sheriff's department and secured the scene," Judith said, brisk. "The first deputies arrived at nine-thirty two. Sophie was still wearing her clothes from last night."

"We knew you'd want all the details," her sister said.

I *did* want the details. But saying it out loud just made me sound nosy.

"Of course," Anabelle continued, "this isn't *your* usual sort of crime. It's random."

I shifted uneasily. "*Was* it random?" Did the sheriff already have a suspect? Arsen shot me a warning look.

"It must have been a hobo or tramp or something." Anabelle motioned to a line of pines against a rise in the mountain.

"You can't say hobo anymore," Judith said sharply.

Her sister tucked her chin. "Can't I? But it sounds so charming."

"Not if the person's a killer," Judith said.

"Do you get a lot of, er, wanderers up here?" I asked.

Judith straightened to her full five-foot-nine-inches. "Certainly not. There's nothing for them up here."

"We did get that lost martial arts group last year," Anabelle said. "They took a wrong turn on a trail and ended up in our backyard. They were doing a retreat."

"They weren't on a trail," Judith said. "That was their problem." She frowned. "Nice folks though. I'd imagine practicing hapkido on uneven terrain would level you up quick."

"Oh, yes," her sister said. "They were very apologetic."

A diminutive woman in a sheriff's uniform strode toward us across the lawn, and I stuffed my planner back into my bag. Curls of golden hair spilled from beneath the sheriff's broad-brimmed hat.

Sheriff McCourt climbed the stone steps and stopped in front of me. She folded her arms. "Figures you'd show up."

"But of course she's here." Anabelle beamed. "Susan and Arsen are going to solve the crime."

Chapter 2

THE SHERIFF'S CORNFLOWER EYES narrowed. "Oh, are they?" A shadow slanted across the brim of her hat and sliced across her pale face.

I winced a little. Sheriff McCourt and I preferred to keep our crime-solving partnership quiet. A Steller's jay fluttered to the low stone wall bordering the patio. The blue bird cocked its head as if curious about what would happen next.

"With your assistance, of course," Anabelle amended with a gracious nod. The sheriff's face pinched.

Arsen's smile was tight. "I think it's best if Sheriff McCourt manage this."

I squeezed his hand. Of course we would investigate. How could we not? But Arsen knew we couldn't make it public we'd be helping the sheriff. And I loved that Arsen and I were in sync about this. It was just one reason why we were perfect for each other.

Though an investigation *would* make it harder to deal with this week's wedding tasks. But plans were made to be revised. I ran my free hand across my oversized purse with my equally oversized planners inside.

Deputy Hernandez approached us on the patio. He ruffled his curling dark hair and replaced his hat.

"But you and Susan have solved so *many* murders," Anabelle said to Arsen. "Really, I don't know how the sheriff would get on without you."

The deputy's mouth quivered. He looked away from the sheriff, whose expression had turned glacial.

My own mouth puckered. Anabelle had never been known for her discretion.

"Susan and Arsen will be too busy preparing for the wedding for that sort of nonsense," Judith said.

Wait. What? My body heated. *Nonsense?*

Deputy Hernandez cleared his throat. "We've taken statements from the others."

The sheriff nodded, her Shirley Temple curls bobbing. "You can let them go."

"Thanks," Arsen said to her, and the deputy strode away.

"I'm not doing you any favors," the sheriff told him. "It's procedure."

"Why would anyone want to kill Sophie?" I asked. She'd only arrived from France yesterday. I hadn't even had a chance to meet her. There hadn't been enough time for her to become a target for murder. "It seems so strange."

"Of course it is," Anabelle said. "That's why it must be a hobo. No one who knew her would want poor Sophie dead."

Judith exhaled sharply. "*Please* stop saying *hobo.*"

"What room did you put her in?" I asked, eyeing Arsen's aunts. My impression had been that the aunts and Sophie hadn't kept in touch. How well did they know her?

"The mountain doors room," Judith said.

"And you're not going in that room until we've gone over it," the sheriff told me. She turned on her boot heel and strode into the house.

"Well that's not very useful," Anabelle said. "How can you investigate if you don't examine Sophie's things?"

"If it was a random crime," Judith said, "what's in Sophie's suitcases won't matter. We should see to our other guests." She angled her head toward the mansion's massive windows. They'd turned to sheets of gold against the morning sun.

Anabelle nodded. "Mimosas, I think." The two older women ambled into the house.

"Arsen," I said helplessly, squeezing his hand. "I'm so sorry." I hadn't known Sophie, but she'd taken care of Arsen when he was young. She'd been a part of his life. But that wasn't the only reason she mattered. Everyone mattered.

He pulled me into his arms. "I know. But you have nothing to be sorry for."

"Did Sophie have any family?" I rested my head on his muscular chest and wrapped my arms around his waist. The fabric of his golf shirt felt rough against my cheek.

He sighed, his chest rising and falling. "I don't know. The invitation was Sophie plus guest, and she didn't bring a guest. I only have vague memories of the woman. Good memories, but vague. At least until the end."

He paused, and I listened to the steady beat of his heart. A squirrel scampered across the rock wall beside the swimming pool.

Arsen sighed. "She left not long after my parents' car accident. Things were in flux. My aunts took over, moving into the house to take care of me. They didn't need an *au pair*. I'm not sure why they invited her to our wedding. Maybe some idea that my parents..." He trailed off.

We held each other. *What a thing to happen.* Even if Arsen only had vague memories of her, she'd been here, alive. And to have that life taken... I pressed my eyes shut. We would find out who'd done this. Sophie deserved that.

Arsen released a long breath. "I should see how my aunts are doing."

"Yes."

But we stood there another minute or two before turning and walking inside. I paused. "I'll meet you in the bar."

He nodded and continued on. I hurried upstairs. Obviously the sheriff hadn't meant it when she'd said I couldn't nose around Sophie's room. She just wanted to keep our relationship on the QT. But I could do that. I'd just be casual.

I walked down the spacious hallway to the mountain doors room. We called it that because its sliding wooden doors had an inset design of blue and brown mountains.

No deputy stood outside the open doors. Feeling more confident, I stepped inside the room.

With gloved hands, the sheriff dug through a suitcase open upon the bed. It was still made-up with a white duvet and blue throw pillows. So Sophie hadn't gone to bed last night.

The headboard looked like an elegant, dark-wood bench shaped like a mountain vista. Except instead of seats, there were two inset thick-wood end tables. To the right was an open doorway. It led to a private seating area containing leather sofas and low wood tables. Floor-to-ceiling windows overlooked the rear of the property and beyond.

A deputy turned from the long wooden chest of drawers. He held up a newspaper clipping. "*The Doyle Times*," he said, "from thirty-some years ago."

The sheriff straightened and noticed me. "Well?" Her lips pressed into a white slash. It was an excellent simulacrum of someone who was annoyed. The sheriff was an amazing actress.

"Do you need anything up here?" I asked innocently. "Coffee? Tea?"

The deputy brightened. "That's—"

"No," the sheriff said.

Glancing around the room, I nodded then returned downstairs. I strolled past a modern, open kitchen and lounge area to the bar. Like so many of the other rooms, it had a spectacular window view, overlooking the pond. But the bar had a high ceiling, extending two-stories.

Three people—a woman seated between two men—sat on cowhide barstools at the distressed wood bar. Behind it was a modern fridge, a wine rack, and all the accoutrements of a commercial bar.

Frowning pensively, Arsen leaned against the other side of the bar, his bronzed arms folded. His aunts were nowhere in sight.

At the sound of my footfalls on the wooden floor, the fit-looking woman with pixie-cut brown hair swiveled in her seat. Nanette Fortin looked to be in her early forties, but she had to be in her late fifties. She and Arsen's father had started up their computer chip business together. Nanette was still running it.

Her smile was grim. "What a way to kick off your wedding week. I'm so sorry, you two."

The two other men turned to face me. They were a study in opposites, Louis Culshaw, the lawyer, silver haired and elegant. Arsen's cousin, Junior Payne, wore a messy, untucked t-shirt. His loose jeans looked like they hadn't seen a washer in a week.

Junior scraped a hand over his thinning hair. "I didn't know the woman," he said pettishly. "I don't know why the police kept asking me about her."

In his late forties, he was over a decade older than Arsen. But he was just as athletic, with broad, muscular shoulders. His blue eyes were piercing, sharklike, against his tanned skin.

"Because she died in a house we were staying in," the lawyer said in a weary tone. Louis was a patrician fifty-something. He wore his white dress shirt open at the collar. A champagne flute filled with orange liquid dangled loosely from his hand.

"She didn't die in the house," Junior said sharply. "She died outside. That's what Judith told me."

"It's a distinction without a difference," the lawyer replied.

"You'd know all about loopholes and distinctions." Junior sneered.

"This isn't about us," Nanette murmured and glanced past me.

Involuntarily, I turned to follow her gaze. On the wall above the seating area were three narrow black and white photos, blown up to at least six-feet tall. They were stripey images of three faces—Arsen's parents and Arsen as a baby.

Every time I saw those images, my heart and throat clenched. This morning my reaction was no different. The aunts kept the photos there in celebration of those lives. But all I could see were two lives cut short, and a baby who had never gotten to know his parents.

"Did you know Sophie?" I asked Nanette in a quiet tone.

"Not well. I met her a few times back in the day." The CEO smiled at Arsen. "John was so proud of you. He'd use any excuse to get someone to drag you into the office. Though usually it was Sophie or Bergdis who'd bring you. They gave you a Norwegian name in honor of your mother, you know."

"Yes." Arsen walked from behind the bar and looked around as if uncertain what to do next.

"Mimosas seem too festive for the occasion," the lawyer, Louis said. "Don't they?" He studied the champagne flute in his hand. "I didn't know Sophie well either. I remember seeing her around this house when you were young. But I'm not sure if we ever exchanged more than a few words. Somehow now I wish we had."

"What is your family going to think?" Nanette asked me, her voice tired.

"My family..." I straightened, my pulse jumping. *My family. My parents.* I checked my watch. They'd be here any minute. I gulped. "Arsen, my parents—"

"Go," he said. "I'll take care of things here."

I hurried around the bar and kissed him. Then I raced away. After all, one doesn't leave semi-retired assassins waiting, even when they're family.

Chapter 3

THERE ARE ALL SORTS of spies in this world. Some are informants. They gather intel on their own government. Then they pass it on to agents out of love, greed, or a sense of what's right.

Then there are the agents. Most of those collect intel from human or electronic resources. And finally there are agents who take a more active role, for example, as saboteurs or assassins. Somehow, my parents had wound up as generalist agents, doing a bit of everything.

It had been a stressful childhood.

The last time they'd come for a visit, things had gone... badly. But I'd thought we'd reached a sort of détente. They would stop being over-protective and controlling, and I'd stop being so defensive. At least that had been the plan.

My mother scanned the foyer of my B&B, twin lines creasing the space between her eyebrows. She wore a blue A-line skirt and floral blouse that made her appear dowdy, hiding the lean muscles beneath. The effect was entirely intentional.

Her gaze landed on the cubby of shelving beneath the stairs. Alien bobbleheads, t-shirts, and books lined the white shelves. A brochure rack promoting the best of Doyle stood near the front door.

"You haven't changed a thing, I see," she said, tone disapproving. More gray threads had appeared in her brown hair. But age hadn't dulled her knife's-edge personality.

I stiffened. "Why would—?" I smiled grimly. *Détente.* "I've put you in the turret room."

She nodded, the colored light from the stained-glass transom shifting across her strong features. "Good view of the court, easy exit through the windows."

"Also," I said, "it's our largest room."

"Anyone die in it?"

My mouth puckered. "No."

"Where's your cousin Dixie?" she asked.

Hiding, if she's smart. Bailey hadn't made an appearance either. "Oh, she's around somewhere," I said with forced cheerfulness.

The screen door bumped open. My father crab walked inside carrying two large suitcases. They could contain anything from formal wear to armaments, and likely held both. He dropped them on the Persian carpet—ruling out nitroglycerin inside—and wheezed.

My mother snatched the room's key card from my hand. "We're in the turret." She climbed the green-carpeted stairs.

He adjusted his glasses, his gray eyes serious. "You two didn't argue already, did you?"

"No. Did you?"

My father grimaced. "Retirement has been an adjustment for your mother. She tried volunteering. It wasn't long before she suspected misuse of funds and embezzlement at the non-profit. Then the spy games began again."

"Oh, no. *Was* someone embezzling?"

He ran a hand over his hair, as thin and sparse as his frame. "Of course they were. Your mother is many things, but wrong is rarely one of them." He sighed. "As she frequently reminds me."

"What happened?"

"The usual. Local politicians were involved. The charity folded." His brow wrinkled. "It's more challenging when you're not under-cover. Now we have to live with people who know what we've done. How do you manage it?"

I blinked. "Me?"

"This is a small town," he said. "After all your investigating, a lot of people must want you dead by now."

"That's— What? No." People didn't want me *dead.*

Well, maybe the people who'd wound up in jail, but they were in *jail.* And okay, maybe some of their friends and relatives, but... I twisted the watch on my wrist. *Oh, dear.*

Bailey burst through the kitchen's swinging door. The beagle galloped to me, his tail wagging. Thinking hard, I bent to pet him. *Did* I have enemies in Doyle?

My cousin Dixie followed more slowly. Her dark hair was tipped with blue. She jammed her hands in the pockets of her olive-green shorts. With her black tank top and sandals, she almost looked like a tourist. "Hey."

My father smiled. "Good morning, Dixie. It's nice to see you again."

The screen door swung open. My father's gaze flicked toward it.

A man in his early thirties and several inches taller than my father ambled into the foyer. His white t-shirt showed off his broad shoulders and olive skin admirably. He grinned. "Susan Witsend around?"

"That's me," I said.

He stuck out his hand, and we shook. "I'm Ghost, Arsen's best man."

"Ghost?" Dixie quirked an eyebrow. "Your parents named you Ghost?"

My insides tensed. Last Valentine's Day, Dixie had been spectacularly ghosted by a guy she'd met online. She didn't talk about it much. But I still felt terrible about it, and I'd had nothing to do with the affair. Ghosting was a sore spot.

"No," Ghost said. "Arsen did. My real name's Estevan."

"A military man?" my father asked.

"Used to be." The two men shook hands. "I'm a bouncer now," Ghost continued.

Dixie rolled her eyes. "It figures Arsen would have friends in the military-industrial complex."

"Ex military-industrial complex," Ghost said. "I mean, I'm ex. The military-industrial complex is still going strong. In fact, it's gone global. Ever heard of the WEF conspiracy?"

Dixie sneered. "You call the World Economic Forum a conspiracy? They've got a website. It lays out their plans to turn the world into an authoritarian hellhole. Photos of the politicians involved are right there."

"What better way to hide something?" Ghost asked. "You put it out in the open, and no one takes you seriously."

My father rubbed his jaw. "There's something to that."

"Sure," Dixie said. "And the X-Files legit described a massive government alien conspiracy. The show was allowed to exist by the government to provide plausible deniability."

Ghost frowned. "You think?"

Dixie's upper lip curled. "Yeah. Click here and win a million dollars." She pivoted on the heels of her black boots and strode into the kitchen.

"Uh," my father said. "What did she mean?"

"She means I shouldn't be so gullible." Ghost watched the arc of the swinging kitchen door slow. An interested smile played at the corners of his mouth. "Who was that?"

"My cousin, Dixie," I said.

"Huh." Ghost shook himself and braced his hands on his trim hips. "Is Arsen around?"

"He's at his aunts' house," I said.

My mother descended the stairs. "Should we go there? I'd like to meet his family."

I clawed back my hair. "Ah, I'm not sure now's such a good time. One of the guests, well... She was killed last night." Hastily, I explained.

"His old *au pair*?" My mother smoothed her blue skirt. "That's okay then. And we'll be too busy with the wedding for you to investigate."

"How is it okay?" I asked, affronted. There was nothing *okay* about murder and especially not of one of my wedding guests.

"I simply mean the murder isn't connected to politics or anything international," she said.

Ghost's head swiveled to study my mother. His dark brow creased.

"It's a shame, really," she continued. "But as I said, we'll be busy. There's only a week to go until the wedding. Of course, when Hank and I got married, it was much more spur of the moment. On-the-run, you might say." She laughed lightly.

My chest hardened. How could she treat this so casually? "Sophie might have *only* been an *au pair* at one time, but she was a guest and a real human being."

"Of course," my father said, his lean face sober. "Her life had value, and no one had the right to end it before its time. Fortunately,

Doyle has an excellent sheriff's department. I'm sure they'll clear this right up."

My nostrils flared. "The main suspects are Arsen's family and closest friends."

"Tricky," my mother said. "And an even better reason for you to let your sheriff handle this."

I jammed my hands into the pockets of my capris so I couldn't curl them into fists. My mother *knew* I hated it when she told me what to do.

When I'd been young, my parents had controlled my every move. In fairness, there had been some spy safety issues involved. But they'd clung to those habits for far too long, and I'd let them. I wasn't going to let it happen again. "That's—"

"I'm starving," my father said loudly. "Let's get out of Susan's hair. I'd like to find that excellent little restaurant we ate at last time we were here." He grasped my mother's hand and half-dragged her outside.

"Just spit-balling here, but there seems to be an undercurrent I'm not locking in on." Ghost frowned. "I'm not saying you need to fill me in or anything. Family stuff stays private. I'm just saying, I'm confused."

The undercurrent was simple. If I hadn't been committed to helping the sheriff before, I was now. It was the principle of the thing. I smiled. "Let's get you settled. Then, we'll talk."

Chapter 4

I GOT GHOST INTO his room and hurried downstairs and into the kitchen. Arsen trudged through the door from the side porch. It banged shut behind him, rattling the white mugs hanging from beneath a cupboard.

At the sight of him, Bailey gave a pleased yip from his dog bed under the table. The vacuum roared upstairs, and my gaze flicked to the white ceiling. Dixie was being unusually conscientious with today's cleaning.

Arsen dropped into the wooden chair across from me, his legs sprawled. Late morning sunlight streamed past the blue curtains in the window above the sink. It gleamed golden on the linoleum at his feet.

"Arsen." I sat across from him. Reaching across the table, I took his hand. "How are your aunts?"

"Determined to get justice for Sophie. I think it's their way of coping. They feel guilty. They were the ones who brought her here. They had to hire a PI to track her down in France. They even paid for her plane ticket."

"They may be on the right track," I said quietly. "Not about feeling guilty, of course. How could they have known this would happen? But about getting her justice."

"I want that too. But..."

I cocked my head. "But?"

"Leaving aside the wandering mountain-man-killer theory, the prime suspects are my relatives and oldest friends. I—"

The door to the foyer swung open. Ghost breezed inside. "Reaper, my man."

I frowned. *Reaper?* Arsen rose, and the two men thumped each other's backs.

"Susan told me about the murder," Ghost said. "Your aunts doing okay?"

"Shaken up," he said, "but they're tough. Fortunately, the sheriff here knows her business. And I owe you a beer."

Ghost laughed. "More than one, dude. What's there to do in this town?"

"I got a few ideas," Arsen said. "I'll meet you outside in five."

Ghost nodded and ambled from the kitchen. I watched the door to the foyer swing shut behind him.

"I need to say hello to your parents," Arsen said.

"They're out to lunch. And they know what's going on."

He pulled me to standing and into his arms. "This was not how I saw our wedding week going. I'm sorry about this."

Investigating *would* tighten up our schedules. But there wasn't any way to get around that. "What happened isn't your fault either." I rested my cheek against his chest.

Moments of quiet togetherness like this had become rare in the rush of wedding prep. And despite the awfulness of the situation, I found myself relaxing against his solidity.

The foyer door swung open. His aunt Judith strode inside my kitchen with a long, white box beneath one lean arm.

"What are you doing here?" Arsen asked.

"I've brought the veil." She set the box on the table. "Had to get out of the house. Cops still underfoot. Anabelle took everyone to the Lakeview for lunch."

Arsen reached for the box.

"Ah, ah." She slammed her age-spotted hand atop it. "Groom can't see it before the wedding day. Tradition."

"I've already seen it in the old wedding photos," he said.

She shook her gray head. "Not the same. Beat it."

Arsen grinned. "I'll see you ladies around." He walked from the room, the door swinging behind him.

"Well?" Judith asked. "Take a look."

I smiled. Judith may have been shaken by the murder, but she was rebounding admirably. Or maybe the veil made a good distraction.

I lifted the lid. Together we drew out the vintage veil, white lace bordering its edges.

"It's beautiful," I breathed. "The restorer did an amazing job." Not a trace of the aged yellowing remained.

"The headpiece is smooth again too," she said. "All the restorer had to do was steam out the wrinkles."

Lightly, I ran my fingers over the ivory comb attachment. "It's perfect. Thank you for this."

Judith cleared her throat. "Bergdis would have been thrilled," she said, gruff. "She would have loved you." The older woman blinked rapidly and looked away.

My eyes heated. It was so unfair that Arsen had grown up without his mother—without both parents. But Judith and Anabelle had raised a good man, and for that I was grateful. Bailey leaned against my leg, his warm weight a comfort.

"You've both been wonderful," I said. "To Arsen, to me..." I trailed off, my throat tightening.

Judith sniffed and raised her chin. "Nothing gives us more pleasure." She lowered her head. "I just wish... I'm sorry this happened. Sophie's death, I mean. I wanted your wedding and everything leading up to it to be perfect. Don't let what happened taint your day."

But a pall had been cast—over everything and everyone. "I never even got to meet her," I said quietly.

Ramrod straight beside the kitchen table, Judith shook her head. "We were just getting reacquainted ourselves. Sophie seemed a lovely woman. A little uncertain, but..." She grimaced. "Maybe she'd always been that way. It had been nearly thirty years since we'd seen each other."

"What did you two talk about?" I bent to pet the old beagle. His chocolate eyes gazed soulfully back, as if he understood the gravity of our discussion.

"The past, mainly. The accident..." The corners of her mouth turned downward.

"The accident? You mean Arsen's parents?" I set one of the wooden chairs more firmly against the small table.

"It was inevitable, I suppose. Not a pleasant topic, but that night changed everything. She was feeling guilty."

"What did she have to feel guilty about?" It had been an accident. Sophie and Arsen hadn't even been in the car, thank goodness, or I might have lost him too.

"Nothing, of course," she said. "She couldn't have stopped Arsen's parents. They left without telling her they were going. And even if they had told her, why would she have stopped them? No one could have expected John to take the turn so fast."

She grimaced. "He did love that sports car. They were planning on getting rid of it—too small for a family." Her face reddened. "They *should* have gotten rid of the thing."

"But Sophie said she felt guilty anyway?"

Judith shrugged. "People aren't rational. We like to think we are, but we're just bundles of emotions and nerve endings. That's what I like about you, Susan. You keep it buttoned up, under control."

I smiled weakly. It didn't always feel that way. And I'd come to realize that emotions were more to be managed than controlled. But I tried.

"Well." Judith slapped her hands on the round table, and the beagle started. "I'd better get to the restaurant and be social. Need help with anything before I go?"

"No, thank you. Everything's under control."

Judith winked. "I'll bet it is." She strode from the kitchen.

I stared at the door swinging slowly shut, and my gaze clouded. It *had* been natural for Sophie to talk about the accident. But why express guilt? And why on earth would someone kill a visiting ex-*au pair* from France? Her only connection to Doyle was nearly thirty years in the past.

The past. Was that why she'd been killed?

Dixie walked into the kitchen, interrupting my thoughts. My cousin jammed her hands into the pockets of her shorts. Casually, she looked around. "I'm done cleaning the rooms. You need any-thing?"

"No." I did a double take. Dixie never volunteered, which meant she never asked if I needed anything. My eyes narrowed. "Why?"

"Because you're getting married in a week. Duh."

"You're still going to be there for our pre-wedding planning review, right?" We were keeping the wedding small. Dixie was my bridesmaid and Ghost was Arsen's best man, and that was it. But several of my friends had volunteered to help with last-minute wedding prep. We were meeting to go over everything this week.

Dixie rolled her eyes. "I'm not bugging out. Just because my love life is a disaster doesn't mean I'm going to rain all over yours."

I bit my bottom lip. "I didn't mean—"

"Don't worry. So do you need anything or not?"

"Not." I'd hoped Dixie had gotten over her Valentine's Day disaster. But she'd nearly gone to Vegas to meet up with the guy who'd catfished her. It had been a big deal for her. Though I suspected the sting of being hoodwinked had hurt more than the broken romance.

"Good." She stomped to the door to the side porch and went outside.

I squatted beside the table. Bailey looked up at me from his blue dog bed. "I'm going out," I said, "but I won't be gone long." I ruffled the beagle's fur. Straightening, I jammed my planners into my purse and left.

If Sophie hadn't been murdered by a wandering killer, then she'd been murdered by someone who'd known her. There'd been a personal reason, and that meant something—*someone*—from the past.

My stomach churned. That might mean one of Arsen's friends or relatives was guilty. On the whole, I preferred the random psychopath theory. But what were the odds?

Driving into town, I parked on the shady sidewalk outside the old town hall. There'd been a fire in it a couple years back, but the town had restored the two-story building, built in the 1890s. I smiled up at the cupola as I walked across the small patch of lawn to its brick steps.

The aging receptionist nodded to me as I crossed the circular marble hall to the winding steps. Descending to the basement, I walked down a narrow hallway. Florescent lights flickered overhead. I knocked on a closed, pebbled glass door reading RECORDS and opened it.

A pasty-faced young man looked up from his desk. "Yes?"

"Is Mrs. Steinberg in?"

His forehead wrinkled. "Uh..."

"Susan." Mrs. Steinberg, in a long black dress and Jackie-Kennedy style sunglasses, stomped across the room, crowded with boxes. She leaned on her thick cane. "What brings you to town records? Never mind. I know. Peter, I'm taking a break."

His mouth puckered. "Wait. Who...?"

I followed the white-haired lady back up the stairs and outside. We stopped beneath an elm tree.

She adjusted the black purse over her arm. "So. Murder. What happened?"

I should have known word would have reached her by now. Mrs. Steinberg knew *everything* that happened in Doyle. I told her what I'd learned so far.

"I remember Sophie." She rubbed her chin. "Pretty young thing. With that French accent, she had all the young men of Doyle spinning."

"Did she have any boyfriends?"

"Derek Anderson. Owns the spice shop. Married a woman from Angels Camp." She eyed me. "You think Sophie may have tried to reignite an old flame and got killed for her trouble?"

"I think... I don't know what to think," I admitted. "Would the town hall have any records of the accident that killed Arsen's parents?"

"Maybe. Why?"

"The accident seemed to have been on Sophie's mind, but maybe..." I smoothed the front of my blouse. It was probably noth-

ing. But if she'd been killed over something in the past, maybe it
was something. "Would you see if you can find anything?"

A squirrel scampered across the lawn. It paused to eye us, then
flicked its tail contemptuously and raced up an elm.

The old lady nodded slowly. "Yes, but you might have better luck
at the newspaper office. If I find anything, I'll let you or Arsen
know."

"Ah, maybe just me for now."

She arched a snowy brow. "Not tell Arsen? What's up? Trouble
in paradise?"

"No," I said quickly. "Of course not. He's just busy with the wedding planning, and it's a little painful for him."

She folded her arms. "Huh."

"Susan?" Anabelle hallooed from across the street. "Is that you?"

I waved back. "I'll be right there." I turned to Mrs. Steinberg.

But she was gone.

Chapter 5

AT LEAST BREAKFAST AT the B&B went off as planned the next morning. But my expectations there had been low. As long as no one got blood on the blue-toile wallpaper, I'd planned on calling it a success.

My parents were unnaturally subdued. That might have had something to do with the sense of calm. On a good day, they were chaos incarnate.

"Pass the scones, will you?" My father yawned. Morning sunlight streamed through the blue-patterned curtains in the octagonal breakfast room. It paled his gray button-up shirt and made starbursts off his watch and the brass lamp above the table.

"You know there's nothing to pass," my mother said, wearily dropping into a high-backed chair. "You take what you want from the sideboard, B&B style." She ran a finger beneath the cuff of her floral print blouse.

His head and shoulders slumped forward. "I'm too tired to process the obvious. I'm done."

"I'll get the scones." Bleary-eyed I rose, my chair scraping over the wood floor. Grabbing the plate from the sideboard, I brought it to the table.

My father studied Ghost, shoveling eggs into his mouth. "How are you so bright eyed and bushy tailed? That rooster next door was crowing before dawn." He turned to me. "Did you give Ghost a quieter room?"

"There are no quieter rooms," I muttered grumpily.

I *really* needed to do something about the new bantam rooster on the block. Guests had left a few comments about him on the review websites. So far, they'd all been written in a humorous vein. But it was only a matter of time before a reviewer lost patience.

"I can sleep through anything," Ghost said cheerfully. "You need to be able to grab shuteye when you can."

My father grunted. My mother glared.

Dixie, in camo pants and an Army-green tank, strolled into the room. "What's for breakfast?"

"Scrambled eggs, scones, bacon, and fruit," I said. There was also toast and homemade Greek yogurt beside the pitchers of juice on the sideboard. True, my parents and Ghost weren't paying guests. But I couldn't bring myself to skimp on breakfast.

My cousin loaded her plate. Ghost watched her movements. "You're not worried about the government putting chemicals in your bacon?" he asked.

"No," she said without turning from the sideboard. "I'm worried about *corporations* putting chemicals in the bacon and a corrupt government turning a blind eye. But Susan only serves organic."

I opened my mouth to point out I only served organic after Dixie had pestered me endlessly. Then I closed my mouth. The guests *did* seem to appreciate the natural touch.

"So what do you think about digital currencies?" Ghost asked her.

"If you're talking about CBDCs—again, not a conspiracy," she sing-songed. "Central banks have been up front about how they want to use digital currencies."

"Yeah, but they're still creepy as hell."

She turned and rolled her eyes. "Tell me something I *don't* know. They say they'll program them so you can only buy things the governments like. As if that's a *good* thing. It wouldn't even be real money anymore. It wouldn't be a store of value. They're talking about linking this so-called currency to a digital ID. It'd be a direct form of social control."

Ghost leaned back in his chair, his gray t-shirt stretching across his brawny chest. His gaze raked her up and down. "You live nearby?"

"Maybe."

His eyes narrowed. He drew breath to speak, but Arsen strode into the room. Whatever Ghost would have said was lost in morning greetings.

Breakfast concluded without incident. Though there *was* an awkward moment when my mother insisted Arsen call her "Mom." And then Arsen and I retreated to the kitchen for the cleanup.

This took longer than it normally would have, because Arsen had other things on his mind. But I was all in on the distraction. Things might have gotten completely out of hand if Dixie and Ghost hadn't stormed into the kitchen.

Arsen hastily released me. I straightened my blouse.

"*Please.*" Dixie glared. "The Rosicrucians were a 17th century practical joke that went too far. And just because they're a secret society now, it doesn't make them conspiratorial. What are they conspiring about? Evolving into shimmering beings of light? Let 'em."

Ghost rubbed the back of his neck. "I'm just saying, there's some weird stuff at their museum in San Jose."

"There's weird stuff in Doyle," she said. "That doesn't make a conspiracy."

He canted his head. "Are you kidding me? What are the odds the government *wasn't* involved in Doyle's so-called UFO abductions?"

"Where are my parents?" I asked before things could go too far down that rabbit hole. Our UFO history might be my bread and butter, but Dixie could go on about it way too much.

They glanced at me. "They've gone to take care of that rooster," Dixie said.

"What do you mean take care..." I felt the blood drain from my face. "Oh, no." I raced onto the side porch, through the yard, and around the back of the Victorian.

My mother stood beside the shed. She scanned my neighbor's yard over the picket fence. She glanced at me. "Now, Susan, before you say anything—"

SQUAWK! A bloodcurdling shriek split the air.

The hairs on my arms stood on end. "Oh my God. You can't kill my neighbor's rooster!" I moved toward the picket fence.

My mother grabbed my arm. "That bird is highly irritating, and your father knows what he's doing."

"That's what I'm afraid of." I made to clamber over the fence.

My father bulleted around the corner of my neighbor's Victorian cottage. Blood streaked his wrist. A blur of red and gold feathers sped after him.

"Oh my," my mother said.

"Save yourselves," my father bellowed and dove over the picket fence. He came up in a neat roll and pivoted.

On the other side of the fence, the rooster clawed the ground. The bird loosed a triumphant crow.

My mother eyed my dad critically. "Hm."

"That's no ordinary bantam." He panted, rubbing his wrist. "There's something wrong with that bird. He tried to eat my watch."

"I'll get the first aid kit." She strode toward the B&B's rear stairs.

"You can't kill my neighbor's rooster," I told him.

"Oh, yes I can. Just because it surprised me this time—"

"I meant you *may* not kill my neighbor's rooster. It doesn't belong to us. Killing it would be wrong."

"That blasted bird is going to ruin your business."

I shifted uneasily. He might be right, but that wasn't why he'd gone after the rooster. "Just let me deal with the bird. It's my neighbor and my problem."

"You have twenty-four hours."

I stiffened. "You can't lay down ultimatums. This is my B&B."

"I know, but that's as long as I'll be able to hold off your mother."

Oh. I glanced uneasily toward my Victorian. A crow landed on the UFO protruding from its mansard roof. "I'll take care of it. Are you coming to the lake?" We'd planned an out-of-towners picnic there.

He sighed. "I suppose we have to?"

"Yes." Because I didn't trust them to be left alone. My father might think he had twenty-four hours, but my mother might have other ideas. "The other early arrivals are going to be there."

"Then I guess we're coming," he said morosely. He brightened. "Maybe we'll get lucky, and one will be an international killer."

"Yeah. Lucky."

Because I could, I left them in Arsen's capable hands. He had the biggest car and would drive them to the lake.

I drove to his aunts' house to collect guests. We caravanned down smooth, serpentine roads to the lake. Our little group reached it before Arsen and the Wits' End contingent. We claimed a spot on a sandy bit of shoreline.

The lake sparkled in the sunlight. Paddleboarders glided between granite islands studded with pines.

Nanette and Arsen's aunts went to see about paddleboards, leaving me with Louis and Junior. Junior shot the lawyer a dark look and moved to the far end of the little beach.

"Is there something going on between you two?" I asked the silver-haired lawyer. Today he was elegant in khaki shorts and a short-sleeved blue button-up shirt.

Louis looked out over the lake, mirrored in his sunglasses. He sighed, his arms folded. "What's between us is thirty years of resentment. Junior thinks his father was treated unfairly when Arsen's parents bought him out of the company. At the time, the company was struggling. Junior's father wanted out. It wasn't easy for John and Bergdis to scrounge up the money to buy his shares. They had to take out a loan to do it. Then the company took off."

"And Junior's father regretted his decision?"

He laughed hollowly. "That's an understatement. He poured all of his bitterness into his son, I'm afraid."

"What about Nanette?" I asked. "Was she involved in the buy-out?"

"Only as much as I was. We were employees." He turned to me and smiled. "Is this an interrogation?"

"I'm sorry. Did it feel like one?" I hadn't thought I'd been that obvious. Besides, Junior might resent the Holidays and Louis. But it was no reason for him to kill Sophie. Though you never knew where intel would lead.

Louis shook his head. "No. Judith and Anabelle have been singing your praises when it comes to solving crimes." He grinned. "Susan and interrogations seem inextricably linked now. But Junior had no reason to resent that *au pair*."

"Sophie wasn't always an *au pair*."

He removed his sunglasses and rubbed the bridge of his patrician nose. "No, I suppose she wasn't."

"Did you know her? When she lived with the Holidays, I mean."

"Not really." He set his glasses on top of his graying head. "I saw her out and about with little Arsen, of course. She must have been bored out of her skull here. Thirty years ago, Doyle was a very different place, much smaller and more insular."

It was *still* small and insular. "But you were here," I said.

A motorboat sped past, weaving between the islands. Waves lapped more loudly against the shore.

"Not so much," he said, "I was based in Sacramento."

"How did you meet the Holidays?"

"I met Bergdis at Berkeley. She introduced me to John." He smiled and shook his head, his gaze growing distant. "They were a remarkable couple. I knew even then that they'd go places."

"Did they get on well with Sophie?" I asked.

His blue-gray eyes widened. "Of course, or they wouldn't have let her care for their only child." He shifted to face me, sand crunching beneath his loafers. "And now you *are* interrogating me."

Insides twisting, I looked at my sandaled feet. "Sophie was invited to our wedding. I feel responsible." I really did, though I knew it was irrational. But she'd been our guest. And she'd only been here because of us.

He patted my shoulder. "You're getting married in less than a week. Let the sheriff do what she's paid for. You and Arsen focus on moving forward with your life."

I exhaled slowly. "I wish it were that easy."

"Isn't it?"

"As a lawyer, you must know that justice isn't always done. We can't just sit back and assume it will be this time."

He smiled. "I understand what Arsen sees in you. You remind me a bit of his mother. Not the looks of course, but the determination. Nanette didn't stand a chance."

A woman's laugh floated through the pines. Footsteps sounded on the dirt trail.

I frowned. "Nanette?"

"Never mind. I shouldn't have said anything." He raised his voice and looked over my shoulder. "How did you fare with the paddle-boards?"

"Success." Judith raised her hands in triumph.

Nanette, in a bikini top and cut-offs, laughed. "But do you dare paddle on said board?"

Louis's eyes twinkled. "I think I can manage."

The older people walked to the shoreline. They toed off their shoes and tested the water.

I rubbed the back of my neck. What had Louis meant to say about Nanette? Stand a chance with whom? Arsen's father?

Nanette waded into the water pushing the paddleboard before her. Her outfit showed off her lean muscles.

I wouldn't want to tangle with the woman. And I wondered if Sophie had found out too late how powerful Nanette really was.

Chapter 6

ALL I WANTED WAS to spend time with Arsen, but there were too many demands keeping us apart. It was more than a little frustrating.

I'd had to abandon him at the lake with our guests while I rushed back into town for our final wedding party check-in. And then I discovered, despite all my planning, I'd messed up the time. Dixie and I were an hour early.

We sat in my car, parked on the sidewalk in front of the red-paned windows of the local coffee shop, Ground. Snapping its pages recklessly, I flipped through my wedding planner. A big truck rumbled past, shaking the Crosstrek.

Dixie shifted in the seat beside me. "I was wondering why we left the lake so early. Not that I mind getting away from all the wedding talk." She sniffed.

I looked up. "You and Ghost seemed to be enjoying yourselves," I said mildly.

I hoped she'd gotten over her Valentine's Day disaster. The best way to get over an old love was with a new one. And even I could see that Ghost was hot and interesting.

Her dark brows lifted. "*Him?* You think I'd get involved with *him* after what happened last Valentine's Day? He keeps pestering me about conspiracy theories that aren't even conspiracies. Honestly, that guy's junior league. And what kind of a stupid name is Ghost? How did he and Arsen become friends anyway?"

I closed my planner and fiddled with its clasp. "Ah..."

Here's the thing. Arsen didn't like to tell people about his time with the Navy SEALs. He wasn't ashamed of it—quite the opposite. But he liked to keep it private. Not even his aunts knew.

I hadn't even known until recently. We'd all thought he'd been bumming around the world working at various resorts. He'd finally started publicizing his experience on his company's website, but it was buried in the *About* section. Apparently, none of his friends in Doyle had bothered reading that part.

"They worked together overseas," I hedged guiltily.

She snorted. "Figures. Ghost *looks* like one of those boneheaded resort dudes. No offense."

"None taken." Arsen had frequently acted like a boneheaded resort dude, even though he was neither.

She squinted out the windshield. "Still... Something seems off about that guy."

"He's only here for the week. After the wedding, you'll never have to see him again."

"Here's hoping." She snorted. "*Digital currencies.*"

It didn't make sense to return to the lake. But I did have time to tick off another item on my list—show that rooster who's boss. My plan wouldn't stop his early morning wake-up calls, but I was playing the long game. This was just step one in the process. "Mind if we stop by Wits' End?"

She shrugged, her seatbelt shifting against her green tank top. "Whatever."

We drove to Wits' End, and I parked in the gravel driveway. Dixie climbed the porch steps and went inside. The screen doors banged.

Leaving purse and planners in the car, I walked to my neighbor's Victorian cottage. I rang the bell. A child wailed from behind the door. Toys lay scattered on the lawn.

After a moment or two, the door opened. My neighbor, Sarah, smiled out at me, a toddler on her slim hip. "Hi, Susan. How's it going?" Her brown hair was tied in a loose knot at the back of her head.

"Good. Good."

She looked expectantly at me.

I swallowed. "So, about your rooster—"

Sarah groaned. "I know. I hate it too. It was supposed to be a hen, and the place that sold it to me offered to take it back. But they'll just kill it, and I couldn't do that to Fred."

"Fred?"

"He reminds me of the character from I Love Lucy. He was always so grumpy. And he hates my husband. He tried to eat his watch the other day while it was on his wrist."

That explained why he'd gone after my father's watch. "Fred must have a thing against time pieces," I murmured.

"What?"

"Nothing." I couldn't exactly admit what had happened. Then I'd have to explain what my father had been doing in her yard.

"Did Fred get into your yard again?" she asked.

"No. But I discovered there's a way to sort of make peace with an aggressive rooster. I was wondering if I could give it a try?"

She laughed. "Knock yourself out. If you can make friends with that bird, teach me the trick."

I walked around her single-story Victorian to the back. A few chickens pecked at the earth around a wood and wire hen house.

The rooster perched on a fence post and glared. Sunlight glinted off his scarlet plumage.

My hand hovered over my watch to remove it. The bird eyed my wrist.

I lowered my hand. No. The watch stayed.

My original plan *had* been to make friends with the bird. But the internet had shown me the error of my ways. One did not befriend a rooster. I needed to become the alpha. And he needed to get used to my watch.

The bantam fluttered to the ground. Fred took a step toward me. He paused, one yellow claw raised.

My insides jittered. All I had to do was grab him, hold his back end to the ground with one hand, and pinion his neck with the other. It wouldn't hurt the bird, and it would make me alpha.

Fred took another step toward me. His black eyes glinted.

I drew a deep breath. *Be the alpha.* I strode toward the bird.

Fred exploded toward me in a blur of red feathers. I shrieked and ran. This wasn't just cowardice on my part. There was no way I'd be able to catch him coming at me like that.

A sharp pain lanced my wrist. I hurdled the picket fence into my yard and turned, panting.

Fred clawed the ground once. Lifting his beak, he strutted away.

I checked my wrist. A thin trickle of blood oozed from the skin beside my watch.

The little jerk had pecked me. I blew out my breath. Next time I'd have to try to catch Fred when he wasn't looking.

"So. That was interesting," Dixie said, one elbow braced on my Crosstrek's roof. "You ready to meet the sisters at Ground?"

My face heated. She'd *witnessed* that disaster? At least she hadn't videoed it and posted it online. "Just a sec." I went inside the B&B and put iodine and a bandage on the scratch.

Outside, Dixie slouched against my Crosstrek. She raised an eyebrow and got into the passenger seat, and the two of us drove into Doyle.

Ground was Doyle's only real coffee shop, so it was a good thing it was amazing. Plants hung from the ceiling and fabric art hung from its distressed brick walls. Spider ferns dangled over the long, wooden counter.

Sunday afternoon wasn't the busiest time at Ground. Only a few patrons sat at its square tables. Three had been jammed together and were lined with silvery gift bags.

The Bonheim sisters, Jayce, Karin, and Lenore hurried to greet us. They were my age, in their early thirties. Though they were triplets, they weren't identical. One had dark hair, one had auburn, and one was a pale blond.

We sat and drank coffee and reviewed the to-do list. My heart lifted. The Bonheims were good people and good friends. I felt cocooned in warmth and goodwill. We discussed the wedding plans and laughed over our drinks.

After an hour, I reluctantly told them I had to get back to my guests. The women helped me carry the tiny silver bags of wedding favors to my Crosstrek. We loaded the bags into the rear.

Mahogany-haired Jayce hugged me, her spring-ivy eyes twinkling. "Are you sure you don't want a bachelorette party? It's not too late."

"I'm sure," I said. "But thanks." I didn't think they'd have planned anything wild. They knew me too well. But you never could tell with Jayce.

I shut the hatchback, and my phone rang in my purse. "Sorry," I said. "I'd better check this."

Jayce winked. "I'll see you around." The three sisters returned inside Ground. Dixie leaned against the blue Crosstrek.

I checked the phone. *Arsen.* My heart jumped. "Hi," I said.

"How'd the big meeting go?" he asked cheerfully.

I glanced at the neat rows of silvery bags in the back of my car. "Everything's on schedule."

"Of course it is." He laughed. "We're wandering down Main Street."

"I'll find you," I said. We said our goodbyes and hung up.

"Well?" Dixie asked.

"Everyone's on Main Street."

Her lip curled. "I'll walk home."

"Don't you want to join us?" I asked, taken aback. Dixie was an important part of the wedding party too.

"No." She straightened off the SUV and strode across the parking lot.

I frowned, a bead of sweat trickling down the back of my neck. Dixie had always been a bit of a loner, and my parents could be a little much. But she was acting more prickly than usual.

I grimaced. And that was her business, not mine. I couldn't control Dixie or anyone else—only myself. Finally understanding that had made my life a lot more relaxing. I made my way around the brick building to the old-west Main Street.

Arsen and the wedding guests ambled along a raised, covered sidewalk. They stopped in front of the ice cream parlor. Everyone but Nanette went inside. She sat on a nearby iron bench, checked her phone, and scowled.

I hurried across the street. "Hi, Nanette." I waved a greeting.

Hurriedly, she rose and slid the phone into the back pocket of her cutoffs. Even in worn denim, a slouchy black blouse, and straw sun hat, she looked elegant and powerful.

She grimaced. "Just checking the office. Sorry." A gust of warm air teased the hair beneath her hat.

"You don't need to apologize." Though it *was* a Sunday. If she was that tied to her work... But who was I to judge? A B&B owner rarely got days off. I could barely believe I was taking a month off to travel around Italy for our honeymoon.

I glanced in the window of the pink ice cream parlor. The group gathered around the counter, chatting and pointing at the menu board behind.

"They'll be awhile," she said wryly. "And I don't do ice cream anymore. How did your meeting go?"

"I think everything's on track."

Nanette laughed. "Even if it's not, the wedding will be wonderful. After all, it's not about the day, it's about what comes afterward." She rolled her eyes. "Says the woman who never married."

"It must have been difficult, taking over after Arsen's parents died." And I hoped I sounded sympathetic rather than nosy.

Her face tightened. "I nearly wrecked everything—twice. We'd put everything into the company. If I'd let it fail, little Arsen would have..."

Nanette's smile was rueful. "But I figured things out. Those were hard lessons." She smiled at me. "And Arsen's not so little anymore."

"How did you and Arsen's father get started?" This was no longer just an interrogation. I really was curious.

Her gaze took on a misty look. "We met in a coffee shop and bonded over our love of tech. We were young. We thought we could do anything. Everything was possible."

Nanette shook herself. "I hear you're wearing Bergdis's gown. I was at their wedding. She was so beautiful. They both were." She studied her leather sandals. "Since I got your wedding invitation, I haven't been able to stop thinking about those days. And now Sophie..."

"Did you know her well?"

"No." Her shoulders slackened, curving inward, her voice dropping. "I probably saw her once or twice with Arsen all those years ago. But I didn't really pay much attention to her. I should have. That was always my problem. I was too much in my head."

The others emerged from the ice cream parlor. "You're here," Anabelle said to me delightedly. The plump woman handed Nanette a small black box. "Show her."

Nanette opened the box and gave Anabelle a look. "Really?"

"Oh, show her," Anabelle said. "She'll love it."

Nanette drew a slender knife from the box. In a liquid motion, she pivoted. There was a blur of metal. The knife quivered in the side of a nearby pine.

"Whoa," I said, disconcerted. Anabelle clapped, her broad face wreathed in a smile.

"One benefit of having money and no social life," Nanette said dryly, "is the opportunity to indulge random hobbies. I can also pick locks." She walked to the pine and pulled the knife free.

"Isn't she wonderful?" Anabelle asked. "Now, let's shop."

Louis staggered and pressed a hand to his chest. "Anything but that."

My mother took the lawyer's arm and laughed up at him. "Oh, Louis. You can browbeat a corporate executive for six hours in court. You can certainly stand a little shopping."

Arsen slipped his arm around my waist. Leaning lightly against his sturdy form, I looked around. "Where's Junior?" I asked.

"He left." Judith's lean face firmed. "Took a ride share back to the house."

"It's difficult for him," Louis murmured.

"Only because he—" Judith pressed her thin lips together and shook her head. "Never mind Junior. We'll have a good time without him."

We split up, the men wandering to the Irish pub and the ladies window shopping. Finally, we agreed enough was enough. Nanette and I walked to my car, while the others went with the aunts in Arsen's big Jeep.

"I'm so glad you invited me," Nanette said as we rounded the brick building. "It's wonderful being a part of a family event again. It's been too long." She stretched.

"And it's wonderful for me to get to know Arsen's extended family."

She stopped short. "Does he think of me as family?"

"Yes, of course."

She blinked rapidly then blew out her breath. "I'm glad."

We strolled into the parking lot, and I slowed. A shredded piece of silver paper skittered past my foot. I bent and picked it up. Another crumpled piece of silver paper drifted along the pavement. I grabbed it as well and wove around an Audi.

"That's so strange—" I sucked in a breath.

My wedding favors lay strewn about my car. The tiny bags were pressed flat, as if someone had stomped them. Broken glass glittered on the pavement.

Numb, I kept walking to the back of my car. The hatchback window was smashed. I stopped short, swaying. *My car. The favors.*

"Oh, no," Nanette said.

I stared, chest heaving, the blood pounding in my head. Who would *do* something like this? To break into my car was one thing. But this wanton destruction—

"Making friends again, young Susan?" Mrs. Steinberg said from behind me.

Chapter 7

AGHAST, I STARED AT the wrecked wedding favors strewn about my SUV. A crow cawed from a utility pole at the edge of the parking lot. I swallowed. "I don't suppose you know who—?"

"No." Mrs. Steinberg handed me a manila envelope. "Here's the information you were looking for. It's good to see you again, Nanette."

Nanette blinked. "Sorry, I... Have we met?"

"It was a long time ago," the old lady said. "A lifetime, in fact. You haven't aged though. Much."

"This is my friend, Mrs. Steinberg," I said, since it didn't appear she was going to reintroduce herself. "She's lived in Doyle for—"

"Long enough." Mrs. Steinberg nodded and thumped away with her cane.

I studied the favors some more, and heat rose behind my eyes. And yes, I *knew* having a crying fit over wedding favors was ridiculous. A woman had been killed.

But we'd all worked so hard on them. How was I going to tell Dixie and the Bonheim sisters?

"Are you going to make a police report?" Nanette asked.

I groaned. What was the point? The sheriff had bigger things on her mind. "There's an online reporting system for crimes like these."

So I took pictures of the car, and Nanette helped me collect what was left of the favors. "I always thought wedding favors were unnecessary," she said.

"The thing is... I hadn't planned on having to replace them," I blurted. Now what was I going to do? This was a disaster.

"Of course you wouldn't have planned for that. Why would you?"

I clenched my fists. I'd planned for everything else. Or at least I'd thought I had. It wasn't fair. I'd *prepared*.

"We should clean up this glass," she said. "Someone might wreck a tire on it."

I nodded. "A friend of mine owns the coffee shop around the corner. I'll ask to borrow her broom."

I trudged to Ground. Jayce, in a black apron, was wiping down the dark wood counter. The brunette looked up when I entered. Her green eyes darkened. "Has something happened?"

"May I borrow your broom? Someone smashed the back window of my Crosstrek."

"Oh, no," she breathed. Her mouth formed an O.

"And..." I steeled myself. "They destroyed the wedding favors," I finished.

Her eyes widened. "They what?"

"I shouldn't have left them in the car," I said rapidly. "I should have taken them straight back to Wits' End. But I didn't think..." I *didn't think*. My heart grew heavy. "Oh, Jayce, I'm so sorry. You and your sisters put so much work into them, and—"

"So did you and Dixie." She hurried around the counter and hugged me. "Of course you can borrow a broom. And a dustpan. Let's go."

Jayce returned with me to the car. Nanette closed the hatchback. She'd retrieved the last of the scattered favors and put them in the rear of the SUV.

"I'm sorry," Nanette said. "I thought we could salvage them, but they're a total loss."

"We can use my scrub," Jayce blurted.

"What?" Nanette asked.

"Sorry," I said. "I should have introduced you. Nanette, this is my friend Jayce. Jayce, Nanette. Nanette's an old family friend of Arsen's."

"My coffee hand scrub," Jayce smoothed the front of her full-coverage apron. "We can give that away as favors. Or something else, like tiny plants. I'll put them in little pots and tie a silver ribbon around them."

"It's too much work," I said. "The wedding's in less than a week."

"Trust me," Jayce said. "We can get it done. I'll draft the guys."

"I'd be happy to help," Nanette said. "I don't think I'm really made for sitting around and relaxing at the lakeshore."

"But..." I hadn't *planned* on coffee scrub. I blew out a breath. And it was a wonderful idea, and my friends were trying to save me. "Thank you. I'll rearrange my schedule, and—"

Jayce gripped my shoulders. "You'll do no such thing. Your schedule is perfect. We can manage this on our own."

"She's right," Nanette said. "You've already got your hands full with the wedding."

"And I'm sure you've got something planned for this afternoon," Jayce said.

"I—" *Oh, crumb.* I *did* have something scheduled. I needed to finalize the seating chart for the reception. "You're right. We'd better get going if I'm going to get you back to the Holidays' house in time."

"I'll find my own ride back," Nanette said. "You go, and I'll organize things with Jayce."

"Thank you both." My eyes blurred, this time with gratitude. "I'll see you later."

I rubbed my bare feet on the furry white throw rug and studied the whiteboard in my parlor. My grandmother had redecorated the room in a modern Victorian style. Now white and black toile paper covered the walls. The couch was black and velvet. She'd added sleek ebony end tables and cabinets. Midnight velvet curtains puddled on the floor beside the windows overlooking the side yard.

My whiteboard provided a pop of contrast. I'd color coded my seating chart using sticky notes—pink for my guests, blue for Arsen's. I wanted to make sure there was a good mix at each table and that no one felt surrounded by strangers.

My father unstuck the sticky note with his name on it from the wedding party table. "I can't sit there. My back needs to be to a wall, and I need to be facing a door." He moved his note to another table.

"It's the wedding party table." I pointed at the long blue rectangle on the whiteboard. "You're the father of the bride. You *have* to sit there."

My mom tapped her chin. "We could move the table."

"It's on a dais," I said. "We can't move the dais."

"There's a window behind the dais," my father said, outraged. "That's no protection from a bullet."

"Who's going to be shooting at you?" I asked, exasperated.

My parents exchanged a significant look.

"For Pete's sake." I snatched my father's pink sticky note off the board and returned it to its spot. "You're retired."

"Semi-retired," my mother said.

My father nodded. "You never know when disaster will strike. Just look at poor Sophie. She'd just gotten her life together, and boom. Dead."

"What do you mean, just gotten her life together?" I asked.

"That's the word," my mother said. "Sophie had a big talk with Junior when she arrived here. She confided that she'd fallen in with a bad crowd after she returned to France and became addicted to drugs. She got clean about a year ago."

"Someone should do something about those cartels," my father said.

"No point," my mother said. "Another waste of space always rises up to take the place of the person who falls. Drugs are a demand problem, if you ask me." She plucked her sticky note from the board and moved it to a far table.

I ran my finger beneath my watch band. "And she told all this to Junior?" He was the *least* sympathetic of the Holiday's guests. Why confide in him?

My father unpeeled a pink note from the board. "You don't want to sit beside Franklin," he told my mom. He moved Franklin's sticky-note to her spot at the head table.

"You can't put Franklin at the head table," I said. "He's not part of the wedding party." He was also a bore. I'd put him beside two elderly and half-deaf great-aunts. They wouldn't have to listen to him. They'd either be asleep or their hearing aids would be off.

Arsen walked into the parlor. He looked exhausted, his broad shoulders slumped beneath his blue, microfiber tee. His handsome face was serious.

"It's the man of the hour," my father said jovially.

"And we'll let the happy couple have some privacy." My mother took his arm and drew my father from the room.

I hurried to Arsen, and he pulled me into a hug. He rested his cheek on the top of my head. "I couldn't do it anymore. Too much family," he mumbled.

"I think surviving the wedding is part of the test. If we can get through the family and the stress, we can handle a lifetime of marriage."

"I just want to be with you. Maybe we can elope."

"With all these guests? Bite your tongue."

"If Sophie..." He sighed and squeezed me a little tighter. "She didn't have any family in France. The sheriff has no one to notify."

My hands dropped to my sides. *The poor woman.* "Did Sheriff McCourt tell you that?"

"She just came by the house. I left her talking to my aunts."

He'd left her? I pulled away. But the sheriff might have learned something important. Puzzled, I studied him. "Arsen," I said slowly. "You don't want to investigate Sophie's death."

"No, I already told you that."

"But... I thought you meant you didn't want to, but you *had* to."

Because he did have to. This was one of his guests, a woman who'd taken care of him as a child. He wouldn't be able to live with himself if justice wasn't done. Running away from a problem wasn't who he was.

My insides knotted. So why was he resisting?

Chapter 8

A LEAD WEIGHT FILLED my stomach. He hadn't meant it—he couldn't. Of *course* we were investigating.

Arsen clawed a hand across his whiskey-colored hair. Afternoon sun knifed through the parlor window. It cast an angular shadow across the white throw rug.

"Arsen." I grasped his hand. "What's going on?"

He blew out his breath. "Nothing more than I already told you."

"It doesn't have anything to do with your parents?"

He stepped away from me. His tanned brow furrowed. "My parents? Why would it?"

"Sophie's only connection to Doyle is in the past," I said slowly, "when your parents were alive." The connection seemed obvious to me. Why wasn't Arsen getting it? Was I missing something important?

"Which is why this murder must have been random," he said. "The best person to solve it is the sheriff."

What? Earlier he'd seemed to think the random-murder idea was ridiculous. What had changed? "But what if it wasn't random? What if her murder is somehow connected to the past, or even to your parents' deaths?"

He blanched. "My parents died in a car accident. Look, I enjoy sticking my nose into a murder investigation as much as the next guy. But not everything is about murder."

"Of course not, but—"

He kissed my cheek. "Look, I've got to get back to our guests. I'm taking Ghost out for happy hour at Antoine's."

I forced myself to smile, but my heart crashed to my toes. He was avoiding the problem. Worse, he was avoiding me.

Lightly, I touched my cheek where he'd kissed me. Was I off base? Or was he avoiding this because deep down, he *did* believe this was about his parents? It was a lot to process. "Don't get in too much trouble."

"Don't worry, we will." He flashed a grin that didn't touch his hazel eyes and strode from the parlor.

I exhaled slowly. I understood denial, maybe a little too well. I'd never seen it in Arsen though. But what if I was wrong? What if it really *had* been a random crime of opportunity?

I shook my head. Maybe it was and maybe it wasn't. But standing around staring at a seating chart wasn't going to answer that question.

I opened Mrs. Steinberg's manila envelope and drew out a glossy eight-by-ten black and white photo. It showed a grainy bend in a mountain highway. I squinted at the lakes in the distance, then I flipped to the next photo.

A red MG lay smashed and overturned at the bottom of a cliff. *His parents' car.*

I turned back to the first photo and frowned. A small pine was broken at the edge of the road. That must have been where they'd driven off. But there were no skid marks. The broken pine was the only sign of the accident from this vantage.

I looked inside the envelope and pulled out a yellowed newspaper article.

CAR PLUNGES OFF 100-FOOT CLIFF, KILLING TWO

—Doyle, CA

Two Doyle residents were killed Tuesday when their car plunged off a hundred-foot cliff on Highway Four, authorities said.

Bergdis and John Holiday were traveling east from their home when their car went off the cliff. It remains unclear exactly when the crash occurred, but it was believed to have been around 6:00 PM, as their nanny reported seeing them leave the house at 5:40. The wreckage was spotted the next morning at 10:23 local time.

The couple were not wearing "safety belts," the Doyle sheriff told the Doyle Times. Both were ejected from the car and died at the scene.

The weather was reportedly clear when the crash occurred. The sheriff's department said it does not consider drugs or alcohol to have been a factor in the crash, though it is unclear exactly what happened. The incident remains under investigation, and autopsies will be performed to determine the cause of death.

I peered inside the envelope again. It was empty. I tilted my head. What *had* the autopsies revealed? Maybe Arsen's aunts would know.

I put the envelope with its contents in my bedroom. Then I collected my things and stepped into the kitchen. My parents weren't there, and a bit of tension seeped from my shoulders.

I didn't exactly sneak out of the B&B, but... Okay, maybe I did sneak out. In fairness, my parents could be a *lot*.

I drove up the mountain to the Holiday's mansion. My excuse would be the seating chart. Not that I should need an excuse to talk to Arsen's aunts. I gnawed my bottom lip. They weren't suspects. They were family.

But when I arrived at the mansion, Junior answered the door. "Oh," he said, "it's you."

Ignoring his bored tone, I stepped inside the modern foyer, with its black and tan marble floor. "Are Anabelle and Judith home?"

He smoothed a hand over his balding head. "No, they're off to happy hour at the Alpine House."

"And you stayed home?"

"I needed a break." His shark-like eyes narrowed.

"Trust me, I get it. I just snuck out of my own B&B to avoid my parents. Not that there's anything wrong with them. But there's a lot going on."

He snorted and turned away. "You have no idea." The big man strode down the wide hallways, and I followed him into the lounge. Walking behind the long bar, he grabbed a bottle of vodka.

I sat on a cowhide barstool. The light had softened, turning the view of the mountain lakes drowsy. "Do you have many memories attached to this house?"

Junior looked around, his tanned face pinching. "This place?" He shook his head and poured two fingers of vodka into a crystal martini glass.

"Sorry, but it seems there's some strain between you and Arsen's aunts. Is everything all right?" I already knew the story, but I wanted to hear his side.

Junior slugged back his drink. "Arsen never told you what happened?" His mouth twisted. "I guess he wouldn't have. It doesn't make his sainted parents look that good."

Sainted? "No," I said slowly. "I guess he didn't."

"My father was a partner in the chip company, until his parents forced him out. Of course, that happened right before the company took off. If my father had stayed in..." He motioned with his empty glass. "Maybe all this could have been ours."

I sat back on my high chair. "How did they force him out?"

"The usual way." He braced an arm on the burnished wood bar. "Why? You think I'm lying?"

"No, of course not," I said soothingly. "This is all just new to me."

"It ruined his life. And mine. He died knowing his own family had screwed him. How do you think that made him feel?"

Bitter, from the sound of it. My stomach hardened. But was it really true?

He snorted. "And then Anabelle and Judith. They lorded it over us from this castle, while they took care of the little prince."

"That's not fair," I said, my blood pressure rising. "Arsen was just a young boy, and he'd lost his parents."

"Yeah, well, he certainly benefited from the company. He still does. And now you do too." His knuckles whitened on the glass.

Fear slivered through me. I slid from the chair. "I'm sorry to hear all this. But thanks for letting me know. I'll let myself out."

But he followed me all the way to the mansion's front door. I didn't relax until I was back in my Crosstrek, the doors locked. Though with the broken rear window, I wasn't exactly protected inside it.

I rubbed my forehead. *Had* Arsen's parents cheated Junior's father? I didn't want to believe it, but I'd never known them, and neither had Arsen. Anabelle and Judith were lovely people though. It was hard to imagine they'd let an injustice go.

I drove back to my Victorian. The Wits' End driveway was empty, aside from my parents' car. Arsen hadn't returned yet. I backed into the drive.

My neighbor's colorful rooster stood perched atop our adjoining picket fence. It cocked its head and glared.

Ignoring the bird, I climbed the porch steps and walked into the foyer. My parents were still nowhere to be seen, probably resting in their room.

Feeling a little guilty now for evading them, I climbed the green-carpeted stairs. I turned at the top of the staircase toward the turret room.

A clunk from inside Ghost's room stopped me. Had Arsen dropped him back off already? Happy hour wasn't even over yet.

I rapped lightly on the door. There was no answer.

I knocked a bit more loudly. "Ghost?"

Silence met my ears. I froze, gooseflesh rising on my arms.

I had not imagined that sound. Someone was inside Ghost's room, someone who didn't want to be caught.

Chapter 9

MY MUSCLES QUIVERED WITH outrage. I have this thing. I *hate* being told what to do. It's not because I'm one of those freewheeling independent women (I never freewheel). It's because my parents micromanaged my childhood.

They *had* to be the ones sneaking around in Ghost's room. Who else would be playing spy but a pair of semi-retired spies? Their invasion of his privacy triggered all my worst instincts. Of *course* I was going to bust in on them.

I waved my master key card over the door lock and thrust open the door. It slammed against the wall and ricocheted back on me. But I'd been expecting that and was already through.

Dixie gaped in front of the bed, the white coverlet's corners tucked military style. She held a pair of sports socks in her hands. "What the hell?"

"What are *you* doing in here?" I sent a mental apology to my parents.

Dixie thrust the socks behind her back. "Nothing. Cleaning."

I glanced around the unnaturally neat room and noted the dearth of cleaning supplies. "What are you doing with those socks?"

She colored. "I... have... a... secret foot fetish."

"Ew. You do not. Put those back."

Carefully, she laid them in the open dresser drawer. My cousin turned to face me, her expression unreadable.

"Dixie, you can't use the master key to spy on guests."

"Why not? He spied on me. He went into my trailer."

"What?" I asked, startled. Why would he do that? "Without you? That's..." *Creepy.* And I couldn't believe Arsen would have a creepy best man. "How do you know?"

Her expression turned cunning. "I've got ways."

"Hidden cameras?" My cousin was awfully good with tech.

"He's a plant," she hissed. "There's something up with that guy. What's Arsen really doing with him? Is he part of a security team or something? Is this about the murder?"

The light shifted inside the Victorian bedroom, a cloud passing before the sun. "Of course not," I said. "They're old friends. And Ghost got here before anyone knew about the murder."

"That *you* know of," she said darkly. "How did those two meet?"

"I told you. Overseas."

"But *how*?"

Oof. "Have you, er, asked them?"

"Yeah. They said they bumped into each other on Arsen's travels. But that doesn't make sense. Ghost *claims* to have been in the military. How would those two have met up at a fancy resort? Something's not adding up here."

One corner of the rag rug had bunched up, and I kicked it flat. Why did Arsen have to be so secretive about his military past? I mean, I got it. I really did. But I didn't like lying to my cousin about it. Especially since my parents had figured it out. It felt like we were keeping Dixie out of the loop.

"Talk to Arsen. I'm sure he'll clear everything up," I hedged.

A door closed downstairs. We shot each other panicked looks.

"They're back," Dixie whispered. She scrunched up the corner of the throw rug with the toe of her boot and shoved me out the door.

Two masculine voices floated up the stairs.

"Your parents," Dixie said hoarsely. She grabbed my hand and dragged me past rows of black and white UFO photos to the turret room. My cousin banged on the door. It sprang open beneath her fist.

My mother looked out. "Yes?" Her mouth firmed.

"Susan wanted to talk to you," Dixie said.

I did? Oh, I had, but now I forgot why. *Right.* Guilt over sneaking out of the house without them. "I just thought we could spend some, ah, time together?"

She folded her arms. "Because you crept out of the house earlier, clearly trying to evade us? It was poorly done, Susan. If there's one thing I can't abide, it's shoddy work."

"Now, now," my father called from somewhere behind her. "There's no harm in her wanting to go off with Arsen. They *are* getting married."

"Arsen left with Ghost," my mother said over her shoulder. "Our daughter was investigating that murder." She faced me. The perpendicular lines between her brows deepened. "I told you this isn't the right sort of case for you."

"Yeah," Dixie said. "But Susan never listens."

My mother rolled her eyes. "You have no idea. When she was a child—"

"Okay." I stepped away from the door. "We're meeting for dinner at five." I hurried down the hall and descended the stairs, Dixie behind me.

We found Arsen, Ghost, and Bailey lounging on the side porch overlooking the gazebo. Ghost looked up from his wicker chair and gazed contemplatively at Dixie. "Hey." He rested his beer on the arm of the white chair.

"Hey back," she said.

"So Black Bart really stayed at the Historic Doyle Hotel?" he asked.

"Black Bart's not conspiracy or UFO related. Don't care," she said, bless her heart. The Historic Doyle Hotel was my main rival. They were constantly rubbing that Black Bart business in my face.

"The receptionist had interesting things to say about the UFO abductions," Ghost went on.

I stiffened. UFOs were *my* purview. What was the receptionist at the Doyle Hotel doing talking about them?

"She said her cousin was one of the returned," he continued.

Dixie sneered. "We call them the Disappeared."

We actually called them the Returned too. But judging from the angry spark in Dixie's eyes, this wasn't the time to bring that up.

"But they all came back," Ghost said, heedless. "So, they're kind of returned now."

My cousin folded her arms. "You can't just go around making up terminology. I suppose you call UFOs UAPs now too."

"Nah." He took a pull of his beer. "UAPs sounds like a government disinformation campaign. Don't trust the new verbiage."

"Huh." She strode down the steps and around the corner of the Victorian.

Ghost stretched and stood. "I'm going for a walk."

Arsen saluted him with his beer bottle. Ghost ambled down the steps and after Dixie.

"What do you think's going on with those two?" Arsen asked.

"I don't want to know. But Dixie was asking about how you two met. She's suspicious of Ghost."

"I told her we met overseas."

"And she's not buying it. It might be time to tell Dixie the truth about where you were all those years."

Arsen reached for me and pulled me onto his lap. The wicker creaked beneath us. "She'll look at me as one of the bad guys."

He might not be wrong about that, but my cousin would get over her prejudice. "What does Ghost think about you keeping this secret?" I looped my arm around his shoulders, and a warm glow of contentment flowed through my veins.

"He thinks I'm undercover. It's cool."

I straightened. It wasn't cool at all. "Dixie loves you. And it's getting hard for me to keep this from her." I hated lying, and I was getting very close to it with my cousin.

He sighed. "Maybe you're right. It's not like Dixie can't keep a secret." His hand moved between my shirt and the small of my back.

"And there's something else." *Actually, a lot of things.* I grimaced. "I saw Mrs. Steinberg today."

"How's she doing?" His broad hand made lazy explorations along my spine.

"I asked her if she had any information about your parents' accident."

His hand stilled. "Why?"

Awkwardly, I slithered from his lap. "I think you should see what she found."

"Sue—"

Before he could complete that thought, I hurried inside. The screen door banged in my wake. Arsen might not be happy with me, but I couldn't keep this from him. He had to see the report.

Stomach jittering, I returned to the side porch with the over-sized envelope. I handed it to him. "It isn't much."

"There wouldn't be. It was just a terrible accident."

"Look at the photos."

He pulled out the photo of the wrecked MG. His face tightened. "I don't think I needed to see this."

A knot formed in my throat. "The other photo," I said gently.

He shot me a look, then extracted the eight-by-ten from the manila envelope. "It's the highway."

"Look at the pavement."

"No skid marks," he said flatly.

"Arsen, could it be—?"

"No," he said. "It's not what you think." The photographs fluttered from his hand to the porch's wooden floor. "I've heard these rumors before. My aunts tried to keep them from me, but it's a small town. I heard."

"What rumors?" I asked, a warm breeze stirring my hair. A bird chirped in a nearby pine.

Arsen's gaze grew distant, his handsome face impassive. One of his hands dangled limp over the arm of the chair. The porch seemed to darken, a cloud sliding across the sun.

His exhalation was ragged. "I really didn't want you to hear this, especially not now."

"Hear what?"

"No skid marks. My father was driving." Arsen paused. "He drove off the road intentionally."

Uncomprehending, I met Arsen's gaze. His hazel eyes crinkled with pain.

"What?" I said. "No, that's not—"

"A murder-suicide," he said heavily.

Chapter 10

IN THE YARD, THE birds had fallen silent, the only sound the soughing of the warm wind in the pines. Condensation beaded the bottle in Arsen's broad hand.

He didn't meet my gaze, his focus on the porch's wood planks beneath his hiking boots. But I didn't think he was seeing his neatly knotted laces, or the spider creeping along the weathered gray wood.

"Why do you think I wanted to hang out with you every summer when we were growing up?" he asked dully. "You weren't from here. You didn't know. Spending time with you was a relief."

I tried to swallow and failed. I thought he'd wanted to be with me back then because he'd liked me. *Another illusion, shattered.* But this wasn't about me. My heart breaking for him, I grasped his hand. "Arsen... I'm so sorry."

He looked up and pulled me closer to his chair. "You have nothing to be sorry for."

My throat ached. "What if... What if that wasn't what happened?"

"Do you think I don't want to believe that? But that's the problem. It's *all* I want to believe. All I've ever wanted to believe was that it was an accident, that my parents loved each other. But I can't trust my instincts on this."

"Maybe you can trust them," I said. "I take it you didn't get a good look at my car when you returned."

He frowned. "No. What happened to your car?"

"Someone smashed the rear window. They didn't take anything. They just wrecked the wedding favors. It happened while everyone was in town."

Arsen's jaw hardened. Rising, he released my hand. He strode down the steps and around the corner of the Victorian. I followed more slowly.

He stood unmoving behind my Crosstrek and studied the broken window. A muscle pulsed in his jaw. "Did you report this?"

"I made an online report."

"The sheriff won't see that."

A spot between my shoulder blades unknotted. He understood.

"We can't say for sure this is connected to Sophie's murder," he said.

My breath caught. *Can't say for sure?* Was he *still* in denial?

"But what are the odds it's not?" he continued, his smile grim, and I relaxed. "Because you didn't let Sophie's death go," he said. "You've been asking questions, haven't you?"

I nodded guiltily. "It just seemed... Sophie was our guest. We brought her here."

He reached for me and pulled me against him. "And we owe her," he said roughly. "Let's talk to the sheriff."

It wasn't as easy as all that. We had to wait until the next morning to see Sheriff McCourt.

She was a busy woman. As her best friend, I knew to give her space to work when she needed it. Also, we'd been stuck entertaining wedding guests for the rest of yesterday.

"So." Sheriff McCourt eyed Arsen and me across her desk.

A Steller's jay on the windowsill rapped the glass with his beak. He cocked his tufted blue and black head like a punk rock star denied his favorite color M&Ms.

The sheriff scowled at the bird, and he flapped away. "You got information for me?" she asked. Her hat tilted precariously on the coat rack near the pebbled-glass office door.

Arsen leaned back in his chair. "Someone vandalized Susan's car yesterday afternoon." He folded his arms over his blue golf shirt, rumpling the logo for his security company. He had a business meeting in Sacramento later that morning and had dressed for the part in khaki slacks.

Her gaze cut to me. "Oh?"

"I made an online report." I shifted in my chair. It was really uncomfortable. You'd think the sheriff didn't *want* visitors to stay and chat. "They broke the rear window and ruined the... what was inside."

She arched a blond brow. "What was inside?"

My body heated. "The wedding favors," I said brokenly. "We've figured out substitutes. Jayce and her sisters are sure they can get them all done in time, but—"

She raised a hand, stopping me. "You sure nothing was stolen?"

"Nothing," I said.

Her pale brows rose. "And you think... what? The vandalization is connected to the murder?"

"Yes," Arsen said. "You know Susan. She's been asking uncomfortable questions of the folks at my aunts' house."

"At your house, you mean," she said blandly.

He blinked. "It's not—Okay, technically, maybe. But practically it's theirs."

My heart stuttered then began pounding hard and fast. The mansion belonged to Arsen? I swiveled in my chair to face him. "What?"

"It was my parents' house," he told me. "Judith and Anabelle moved in after my parents died to take care of me. It made sense for them to stay. To all intents and purposes, the house is theirs."

"It's got to be worth, what?" Sheriff McCourt asked. "Ten million? More?"

"I don't know," he said impatiently. "What does it matter?"

"She thinks Sophie's murder has to do with your parents' deaths too," I said in a low voice. Of course she did. The sheriff and I frequently thought along the same lines. It was why I'd become a critical part of her investigative team.

His brows sloped downward. "Which has nothing to do with my aunts."

"Sophie's only connections to Doyle were in the past," the sheriff said. "We're looking at all possibilities."

"How was Sophie killed?" Arsen asked.

She studied him. "A fractured skull. She was bludgeoned with a blunt object. We haven't found the object in question yet, but the coroner suspects a golf club."

I started. *Golf club?* Both Judith and Anabelle golfed. They had their own course. But I suspected it wouldn't have been difficult for a guest to get their hands on a club. "What about time of death?"

The sheriff shifted in her executive chair, and it creaked beneath her. "We've narrowed it down to sometime between nine PM and midnight on Friday."

Arsen nodded. "That makes sense. She was still wearing her clothing from Friday when Judith found her the next morning. What else can you tell us?"

Her brows lowered. "It's not my job to tell you anything. What have you two heard?"

I told her everything I'd learned and I suspected. She sat in silence for a long moment, her chin propped on her fist.

"All right," she said. "You can go."

Since we'd set the appointment with *her*, dismissing us seemed a little silly. But if she needed to maintain the illusion of control even when we were alone, that was fine by me.

We left. Arsen dropped me back to Wits' End then drove off to his appointment in Sacramento.

I reviewed my planners in the kitchen. Aside from the hiccup with the wedding favors, everything for the wedding was on track.

But an odd feeling hollowed my gut. I'd spent so many hours working on the wedding preparations. And now I had free time. So close to the big day, it seemed like a mistake.

Of course, I'd *planned* for the free time. I'd intended to spend it with our early-arriving guests. If that time now involved investigating those guests, that was that. I closed my planners and pushed back the wooden chair.

Ghost slouched into the kitchen and yawned. "Hey. How'd it go with the sheriff?"

I blinked. "You knew?"

"Arsen mentioned you were going to see her." He leaned against the butcherblock counter. "What are you up to for the rest of the day?"

I rose. "I thought I'd go up to the house and socialize with our guests."

"Cool. I'll come with you."

My gaze flicked to the white-painted ceiling. I couldn't have Ghost hanging around. How was anyone going to spill secrets with a musclebound ex SEAL lurking?

"Oh," I said, "you don't have to. You must have better things to do than hang out with my family."

"Nope." He folded his arms, his biceps bulging, and crossed his legs. He wore khaki slacks with lots of pockets, and I wondered if it was an ex-military thing.

"You don't want to go hiking?" I asked, hopeful.

"Sure I'll hike, if you take me."

I sighed. Ah. "Did Arsen ask you to keep an eye on me?"

"Yep. Besides, I want to hear all about you and Arsen."

I gathered my planners off the table. "No, you don't." Ghost didn't exactly strike me as the gooey romantic type. But I appreciated the effort.

"I don't?" He quirked a brow.

"I have a better idea. You can help me with the escort cards."

He blanched. "What?"

"They're cards that tell people where they're seated, so they can find their tables." I'd been waiting to print them out until I had the seating chart finalized.

"Oh. What do I need to do?" he asked uneasily.

"Only cut and fold them." I'd bought a top-of-the-line paper cutter just for that purpose.

He ruffled his near-black hair. "Fine."

"They're in here." Planners beneath one arm, I led him into the black and white parlor.

I opened the file on my laptop atop the low, ebony coffee table and double-checked the white board. My mouth tightened. My parents had moved people around again.

"Unbelievable." Fuming, I unpeeled Ghost's name from a table at the back of the room and returned it to the head table.

He grasped my wrist and quickly released it. "Uh, can you put me back where I was?"

I turned to him. "Don't tell me you messed with my seating chart too? Do you have any idea how long it took me to put everyone at the right table?"

He shifted his weight. "Yeah. Uh. The thing is, I'd really rather sit with my back to a wall."

"Oh for Pete's sake. I promise you, no assassins will be crashing my wedding." After all, my parents weren't crashers. They were guests. Though I was starting to regret their invitation.

"I know it's unlikely," he said. "But I'd rather sit somewhere else."

"You're Arsen's best man. You have to be at the head table. And there *is* a wall behind it."

"Windows, not a wall," he said darkly. "And they're not bullet proof."

I smothered a groan. Had he and my parents been exchanging notes? "You're sitting with Dixie at the head..." I studied the head table and frowned. Dixie's sticky note wasn't there. Where had it gotten to?

I finally found it at the table in the back where Ghost had moved his blue note. "Honestly," I said. "The reception is three hours, tops. I don't know why everyone's making such a big deal over a seating chart."

"In fairness," he said, "*you're* kind of making a big deal..."

My eyes narrowed.

Ghost cleared his throat. "Er, how do you want those cards cut?"

Chapter 11

"I T'S A STRAIGHT LINE," I said, exasperated. In the parlor, a pile of creamy white cards jumbled at odd angles by Ghost's elbow.

He was an ex-Navy SEAL. He could hit a target at a hundred yards. You'd think folding a card in a straight line would be easy. But the escort cards were *all* crooked.

"You just line up the corners," I said, standing behind him at the card table. "Then you run the bone knife from the middle to one edge, and then from the middle to the other edge."

Ghost dropped the slim, ivory-colored blade to the fluffy white rug. Bailey raised his head, realized it wasn't food, and sank his head to the edge of his dog bed. With a grunt, Ghost bent and retrieved the knife.

Dixie stuck her head in the parlor door. She scowled and retreated.

"Fine." I blew out a breath. "Let's do something else."

Ghost straightened in his chair. "I can help taste test the menu."

Nice try. Everyone wanted to help with that. "That was done months ago. I have to go to the newspaper office."

"Dropping off a wedding notice?"

"Only big-city socialites do that. This is Doyle. Everyone knows Arsen and me are getting married."

Ghost stood and stretched, his t-shirt taut across his muscular chest. "I'll come with you."

"I figured." It would be fine. Subtle interrogation wasn't required at the *Doyle Times*, so it wouldn't do any harm if he tagged along. Jamming my planners into my big purse, I strolled into the kitchen.

Dixie lounged in a kitchen chair and studied her computer tablet. Her tanned legs stretched out at the side of the table. She didn't look up as we entered.

Ghost slowed. "We're going to the newspaper office. Want to come?"

"Nah," she said. "I've got some research to go through."

"Research?" He edged around her to look at her screen.

She flattened the tablet against her tank top. "Local stuff. You wouldn't be interested."

"I might be. What have you got? Radio signals? I've got some experience—"

I cleared my throat. "You know, I'm only going to the newspaper office. If you'd rather stay here—"

"No, no," he said. "I'll come. See you around, Dix."

"Not if I see you first," she said, smiling.

He followed me to my Crosstrek. "So what's the word on your cousin?" he asked casually, opening the door for me.

"She's a brown belt in a martial art I can't pronounce, she once stole a police car, and she hates authority. What else do you want to know?" I leaned one elbow on the roof of the SUV.

His coffee eyes crinkled with laughter. "She stole a police car? Really?"

"Well, a sheriff's department car. Also, our grandmother practically raised her. Since I spent my summers in Doyle at Gran's, we became close."

His dark brows sloped downward. "Why did your grandmother raise her? What happened to her parents?"

I got into the car and fastened my seatbelt. "Nothing. They're still around."

"Huh." He closed my car door and got in on the other side.

"Dixie said you broke into her trailer."

He shot me a startled look.

"I haven't said anything to Arsen." Yet. "Because I assume you have a good explanation that does *not* involve being a stalker. I'd like to hear what it is." I started the car before he could think about getting out.

"I didn't mean to break in. Her door was unlocked."

"I find that unlikely." A woman as suspicious as Dixie wasn't in the habit of leaving her door open.

"So did I," he said, "which is why I went inside. I thought something might have happened to her. But when I realized the place was empty, I left and locked the door behind me."

"Hm." It *could* have happened that way. Dixie was cautious, but everyone slips up on occasion. I backed the car from the driveway, my tires crunching on the gravel. "Have you got any good stories about Arsen?"

He regaled me with a story about Afghanistan he found hilarious. I found it horrifying. I knew Arsen was a risk taker. It was one of his more terrifying qualities. But it was still startling to hear about this particular exploit.

We pulled into the newspaper's parking lot, Ghost still chuckling about a goatherd. "We were all surprised when Arsen decided to move back to a small town, especially after that job offer. Doyle didn't seem in line with his high-risk lifestyle. But I get it now." He smiled at me.

My stomach fluttered disagreeably. "Job offer?" Why was this the first I was hearing about it?

"Head of security for some multinational. He would have had it all—big city life and lots of travel. But he said no. He wanted the quiet life. Of course it was you he really wanted. We all knew the score. He talked about you a lot. I mean, a *lot*."

"Oh," I said faintly. He'd given up an international career for me?

The newspaper office was in a two-story, brick building. We climbed the steps and walked inside, pausing in a paneled hallway. A narrow staircase rose in front of us. Desks, piled high with documents, packed the room on our left. Documents and maps papered its pale-yellow walls.

Tom Tarrant, newspaper reporter and all-around irritant, looked up from his cluttered desk. He waved. "Hey, Susan. You here to comment on my latest podcast?"

Since I hadn't listened to it, *no.* "I'm here to do some research."

He rose and made his way around his desk. "I can help with that. What are you researching?" His gaze flicked to Ghost, towering over me.

I pursed my lips. If I told the reporter, he'd put two and two together and it would be all over Doyle. I doubted the editor would let him speculate on the pages of the *Doyle Times.* But Tom still had that dumb podcast.

I smiled. "We're putting together a surprise for Arsen. It's a poster board for the wedding. I'm looking for stories about his parents."

"This is a little last minute for you, isn't it?" the reporter asked. "I'd have thought you'd have had this squared away months ago."

"It was my idea." Ghost folded his arms.

Tom was an ex high school football player and looked like an all-American jock. But when Ghost crossed his arms, it was a whole other level.

Tom shifted his weight and shot another uneasy glance at Ghost. "You'll want the microfiche room. I'll show you the way."

We followed him to a cramped room. Three carrels held old-fashioned microfiche machines. Windows high in the walls permitted little natural light.

He walked to a cabinet with short, narrow drawers. "What year and month are you looking for?"

"I'll have to check my planner." I adjusted the heavy purse over my shoulder. "You don't have to help us. We can take it from here."

The reporter leaned against the cabinet. "That's okay. I'm happy to help out what with everything your family must be going through. The murder, I mean. I understand Judith Holiday found the body?"

I rolled my eyes. "I don't know anything and wouldn't comment if I did."

"Yeah, well, if you need any help—"

"We don't," Ghost said.

Tom grimaced and slithered from the room.

"I don't like that guy," Ghost said.

Neither did I. But at least I knew now I could trust Ghost's instincts. I strode to the cabinet and ran my fingers down the date labels, stopping in November of the year Arsen's parents had died. I handed him October.

"What are we looking for?" he asked.

"Anything about his parents."

Ghost shrugged and went to a microfiche machine. He easily threaded the film. I don't know why he was so incompetent folding escort cards. He obviously had *some* dexterity.

I sat at the carrel beside him and threaded the November film. Starting at the end of the month, I worked my way backward. My eyes were burning before I found what I wanted.

Sheriff's Department Seeks Answers in Deadly Crash
—Roger Hammer

The Doyle Sheriff's Department is looking for answers after a deadly crash on Highway 4 took the lives of two Doyle residents. John and Bergdis Holiday were killed when their car went off the road on Tuesday evening.

An autopsy determined they died of multiple blunt force trauma, most likely due to the crash. But it was still unclear what caused the accident on the mountain road, which was free of ice and debris.

A visitor at the house from earlier in the day told deputies that the Holidays had been behaving normally and had not, to his knowledge, been drinking.

According to the Doyle Sheriff's Department, more details will be released once they've completed their investigation.

More details later? *Augh.* I'd been working backward, and I hadn't seen any details that had been released. And I knew I hadn't missed anything.

I printed the article. Then I reviewed the December microfiche, and then January's. But I didn't find anything more on the Holidays.

"Did you find anything?" I asked Ghost.

"Nope." He leaned back in his chair, his hands laced behind his head. "What's this really about?"

"Sophie's murder, of course. If it wasn't a random crime—and I can't believe it was—then that means it was personal. And that means something from her past, here in Doyle, was the motive for her murder. The only dramatic event that she was involved in—if only peripherally—was the accident." I frowned. "At least it was the only thing that I know of. She left Doyle almost immediately afterward. The deaths of Arsen's parents could have nothing to do with anything, or—"

"It could be connected to her murder," Tom said from the doorway.

Briefly, I closed my eyes.

I *really* didn't like that guy.

Chapter 12

"WHAT DO YOU KNOW about Sophie Gagnon's murder?" the reporter demanded, walking into the microfiche room. Afternoon sunlight slanted across Tom's all-American face. Dust motes spiraled over the wooden cabinet drawers. "Does the sheriff think her murder is connected to the Holidays' deaths?"

"Maybe you should ask the sheriff for a comment." Ghost leaned back in his chair and folded his arms over his chest, muscles bulging.

"She won't give me one," Tom complained.

"Then there's your answer," I said testily. It wasn't that I had a thing against the press. But Tom had once attempted to seduce information about a murder investigation out of me. The memory still stung.

"You lied to me," Tom said. And though that accusation probably shouldn't have bothered me, it did.

Here's the thing. In the past, I might have had a few *tiny* problems with separating truth from imagination. It was hard sometimes to know what was real. But I'd found that it was a lot harder if I wasn't honest.

Because of that, I'd made a pledge to myself to keep it real. But I'd broken it in the newspaper office.

"I can't discuss it." I removed the microfilm from the machine. My chance of discreetly investigating the past had vanished. "It's a private family matter."

Tom snorted. "Yeah. Judith and Anabelle pulled that line back in the day to shut the old sheriff up."

I sucked in my cheeks. What was *that* supposed to mean? "What are you getting at?" I rolled up the film.

"I mean they squashed the accident investigation and any reporting on the Holidays' deaths."

Heat rose in my chest. "How do you know that? You weren't even born then."

"When I first came to work here," Tom said, "there was an old newspaper man still on staff. He trained me up. He told me all about it."

"Who?" Ghost asked.

The reporter glanced at him. "Roger Hammer."

"Where is he now?" I asked.

Tom shrugged. "Retired. He's living the dream in that old cabin by Mosquito Lake."

I shuddered. It was more pond than lake, but the mosquito part was accurate. That place was a blood bath no matter how much repellant I doused myself with. And it was my blood.

"The sheriff thinks Sophie Gagnon's murder wasn't random then," the reporter mused. "She was killed because she knew something."

"I don't know what the sheriff thinks." I stuffed the articles I'd printed into my slouchy purse, and Ghost stood.

Picking up my planner, I clasped it beneath one arm. "I was only indulging my curiosity. If the sheriff was interested, she'd be here going through your microfilms herself."

"Then you're saying the sheriff *doesn't* think the murder is connected to the past?" Tom cocked his head.

My neck stiffened. "I told you, I don't know what the sheriff thinks. I don't speak for the sheriff."

"Everyone knows you're her little helper." Tom sneered.

Well, that was just insulting. I mean, it was true, but the way he'd said it had been extremely dismissive. "I have no idea what you're talking about." Head high, I strode from the office.

Ghost trailed after me. "Want me to take him out?"

I laughed. "Tom's not worth the hassle." But I bit my bottom lip. How much of that speculation would make it into his next podcast?

"What next?" Ghost asked when we reached the pavement outside.

I stopped in the shade of an elm. "You haven't had much chance to enjoy the local scenery. We could—"

"Mosquito Lake?" Shadows dappled Ghost's chiseled face.

"Yeah," I said, sheepish. Had I been that obvious? "Do you mind?"

"No. I like a good mystery." He eyed me. "Is there something between you and that reporter?"

"No." I walked to the SUV and opened my car door. "Why?"

"You seemed tenser than the situation warranted. I mean, I get it. You don't want all that stuff about Arsen's parents splashed around town. But you tightened up as soon as you laid eyes on that guy."

Ghost was disturbingly observant. Dixie would have to watch herself around him. "Can I just say he's not the most ethical person and leave it at that?"

"Sure. It's your business."

Relieved he wasn't going to press, I got inside my car. We drove out of Doyle and up the narrow highway.

Lakes glinted between the pines as we flashed past. Granite islands gleamed bonelike in the Monday afternoon sun.

"Damn, it's beautiful up here." Ghost studied the sweep of mountains. "I get why Arsen came back. Though you were a big part of that equation too." He flashed me a grin.

I was just glad Arsen *had* returned. But was Arsen? That international job offer... There was so much I'd taken for granted about his life, his opportunities, his money.

We crested the summit and began the descent. I pulled the car off the road at the side of a small lake. On the opposite shore stood a ramshackle cabin. A man sat on its dock and fished.

"How do we get over there?" Ghost asked.

I rolled down the cuffs of my blouse. "There's a trail."

"How does he get supplies in?"

I stepped from the car. "There's a gated road. I'd rather stay off it." It was marshy and where most of the mosquitos seemed to hang out.

Ghost met me at the back of my Crosstrek, and I opened the hatchback. Arsen had covered the broken window with thick, clear plastic. I pulled Arsen's emergency kit toward me and unzipped the canvas bag. From it, I handed Ghost a can of mosquito repellent.

He grunted. "I like a girl who comes prepared."

"Arsen can take credit for the emergency kit." I handed him a water bottle. The trail wasn't long, but better safe than sorry.

We doused ourselves in repellent. After a few minutes of bumbling, I found the trailhead, and we started off. We hiked down the looping path skirting the lake and emerged from the pines near the dock.

The fisherman glanced over his shoulder. "This is private property," he shouted.

I stopped beside a gravel track and swatted my neck. My palm came away bloody. "Mr. Hammer?"

He adjusted his fishing cap and twisted in his chair. "Yeah?" he asked warily.

A mosquito buzzed past my ear, and I flinched. "I'm Susan Witsend. This is, ah..."

"Estevan Rodriguez," Ghost said.

"We wanted to ask you about the Holiday's car accident." Suddenly, I realized we'd driven past the accident scene on our way here. The thought made me a little queasy.

He set his pole in a clamp of some sort and walked down the dock, his sandals slapping the wood planks. "You're the girl marrying the Holiday boy. This have to do with that French woman's murder?" His potbelly stretched the front of his *Gone Fishing* t-shirt.

"I don't know," I said and glanced down. A mosquito had landed on the back of my hand, and I slapped it. "What do you think?"

His wrinkled face scrunched. "I've been wondering about it myself." The fisherman stopped five feet from us and studied Ghost. "Who'd you say you were?"

"Estevan Rodriguez. A friend of the family."

"Military?"

Ghost swatted a mosquito. "Not anymore."

"What do you remember about the accident?" I asked. Something tickled my forehead, and I smacked myself hard enough for it to sting.

Mr. Hammer's thin lips pursed. "It was a bad one. Obviously, both were killed. Their deaths shocked the whole town. The Holidays were so young, and they had a boy."

"Was there anything unusual about the accident?" Another mosquito buzzed around my head.

Mr. Hammer rubbed the back of his neck. "You sure you want to go there?"

Did I? But Arsen had to know. "We need the truth," I said quietly.

The old reporter looked away from me, squinting at the sun lowering above the lake. "I don't know the truth. No one does."

A cloud of bugs emerged from behind a rusted pickup.

"Tom Tarrant said there were things that weren't reported," I said. "Things that were suppressed."

"Nothing was suppressed," Mr. Hammer said sharply. Then he sighed. "There were questions. We didn't report them, because questions was all they were. Our editor at the time insisted on sticking with the facts. Not like reporters today. Their opinion masquerades as news. Innuendo is disguised as truth," he said in a disgusted tone.

"What sort of questions?" Ghost asked.

"It was unclear from the autopsy whether all the blunt-force trauma the victims experienced came from the accident."

"Most likely due to the crash," I murmured. Most *likely, but not definite.* The cloud moved purposefully toward us.

"What?" Mr. Hammer asked.

"The article I found," I said. "It said the blunt force trauma was most likely due to the crash. *Most likely* seemed an odd turn of phrase."

Mr. Hammer nodded. "The road was clear. It was getting dark when the car went over. But they'd driven that stretch of highway many times before. The curve wouldn't have been a surprise."

But if that murder-suicide theory was correct... "Was there anything else?" I asked. The cloud of mosquitos hovered above a weedy section of pond, and I relaxed a bit.

He shook his head. "No. And that's why we didn't go any further speculating."

"Your article mentioned a visitor at the house the day of their death," I said. "Do you remember who it was?"

He squinted at the darkening lake. "One of their work colleagues, I believe. I don't remember the name."

I hesitated. "Was it only your editor who didn't want this to get around? Or was anyone else involved in keeping these suspicions quiet?"

"They weren't suspicions. Just questions."

"And the Holiday family? They didn't have any talk with the editor about it?" I asked. *Tom. Of course* he'd exaggerated. Why had I listened to him?

"They were worried about the boy," the reporter said. "What their son might hear. I can't blame them."

My heart sank. "So Judith and Anabelle *had* put pressure on your editor. Did they pressure the sheriff too?" The mosquito cloud abandoned the lake and drifted toward us.

"*That* one." Mr. Hammer's lip curled. "That sheriff was all about going along to get along. He was useless, if you ask me. We're lucky we finally got a pro in the job who gives a damn."

My stomach turned queasy. They *had* gotten to the sheriff. "Thank you," I said faintly. I gave him a card for Wits' End. "If you think of anything else, would you give me a call? It's important."

"You sure you want to dig up these old skeletons?"

"I'm surprised you don't," Ghost said, "an old newspaper man like yourself."

"I've done plenty of digging in my time. It didn't always work out for the best." The man pocketed my card and returned to the dock.

The mosquitos chased us back to the car.

We drove back to Wits' End not saying much. I pulled into the Victorian's gravel driveway, and we stepped from the car.

I checked my arms. Half a dozen red bumps had begun to swell. Ghost appeared unscathed.

"You're not trying to lose me now, are you?" he asked.

"No." I shut the car door. "It was actually nice to have you along."

His smile broadened. "Glad I didn't screw up your investigation." He quickly sobered. "Though there's nothing funny about this murder. You've been managing it well. Or at least you seem to be. You okay?"

"I'm supposed to be entertaining family today. Instead, I'm interrogating reporters and haunting newspaper offices. I'm fabulous."

Ghost laughed, then squinted. "Speaking of family, aren't those your parents?" He pointed to the side of the yard.

A shadow from the roof's UFO darkened the figures of my parents. They stood beside my neighbor's picket fence. My neighbor with the rooster.

Dread pooled in my stomach. "You know, I should probably go talk to them."

"Gotcha. Family time. I'll see you around." He ambled into the B&B. The screen doors banged in his wake.

I hurried across the lawn to my parents. "What's wrong? What's happened?"

"Eh, nothing." My father turned and smiled. "The sleeping pills work. We just have to get the timing right."

My pulse jumped. "Sleeping pills?" I stepped up to the picket fence.

Chickens staggered drunkenly about my neighbor's yard. One gave a squawk and collapsed to the ground.

I stared, horrified. My parents had roofied the chickens.

Chapter 13

"WHAT DID YOU DO?" I whispered, horrified. The rooster made a graceful pirouette and sank to the ground. I glanced toward my neighbor's Victorian cottage. *Drugs?* How *could* they? This was a nightmare.

"Your father already told you," my mother said briskly. "Sleeping pills. We ground them up and put them in the feed."

My chest tightened. "You can't..." But they clearly could and had. "What are you thinking? Those aren't my chickens! This is vandalism or animal abuse or something."

"Nonsense," my mother said. "We calculated the dose quite precisely. No chickens were harmed."

"You can't know that. And what do you mean you were precise? Dad just said the timing wasn't right. What's my neighbor going to think?"

"She hasn't noticed yet," my mother said. "And she won't if you lower your voice."

"They look drunk," I hissed.

My mother folded her arms. "You *did* say you didn't want the rooster killed. What other option did we have?"

"There are plenty of other options," I said hotly. "You could do nothing. Accept the situation. Try to be a little less murdery for once in your lives."

"We aren't murderers." My father gave me a reproving look.

"Susan?" my neighbor called.

"Oh, crud." I turned toward the picket fence.

"I *thought* that was you." Smiling, Sarah strolled toward us. She stopped short. "What... What's wrong with my chickens?"

"Is there, er, something wrong?" I asked.

"They can barely stand." She picked up a limp white bird. "Edwina? Are you feeling bad?"

"*Brrraapp.*" The chicken's head lolled.

"Oh, no," my neighbor whispered. She hugged the lump of feathers to her chest. "Did you notice any strange birds hanging around? It could be avian flu."

What constituted strange birds? Birds were everywhere. "Ah, no. My parents..." I turned.

My parents had vanished. *Nice.*

"I'm going to call the vet." Gently, she set Edwina down.

No. My heart lurched. The vet would figure out what happened. The neighbors would be the first suspects. And *we* were the neighbors. "You know, I think I've heard of this happening around town," I said. Beads of sweat formed on my brow.

"Then it *is* bird flu." She gasped.

"No, no, it's heat. This unusually warm weather is getting to the, er, chickens. And only chickens. All over town. Maybe if you move them into the shade, or better, into the coop, they'll perk up."

"I guess it wouldn't hurt to give them an hour and then decide on the vet." She worried her bottom lip. "If they think it's bird flu, they'll kill them all."

My gaze darted around the yard. How long would it take for the sleeping pills to wear off? "Exactly. An hour or even two won't do any harm."

"Would you mind helping me move them?"

"Ah..." I wasn't a huge live-chicken fan. But since my parents were to blame, helping her move the birds was the least I could do. "Sure. No problem."

I clambered over the low fence separating our yards. Gingerly, I picked up a chicken and carried it to its coop. And I'm sure I imagined the resentful look in its droopy eye.

We settled the chickens in their coop. Frowning, Sarah picked up a tin of feed. "I'll leave this inside in case they get hungry. It's weird they didn't finish it."

I sucked in a sharp breath. *The feed.* It was still drugged. As if someone else were controlling it, my arm flew up and knocked the tin from her hand. Bits of yellowish feed went flying.

She gaped. "What did you do that for?"

"I don't know," I said wildly. "My arm just... spasmed."

"For no reason?"

"Ah... The thing is..." What was the thing? "The wedding's been making me a little jumpy."

She cocked her head, her brow wrinkling. "Of course. That woman's murder. I'm so sorry. What an awful thing to happen to one of your guests. Were you two close?"

Her sympathy only sharpened my guilt. "No, Sophie was one of Arsen's guests. His old nanny."

A child's wail emerged from the cottage, and she smiled faintly. "What I wouldn't do for a nanny. Thanks for the help." She hurried into her house.

I scuffed dirt over the fallen feed then returned to Wits' End. My parents lounged in my kitchen drinking coffee around the table as if they hadn't a care in the world. Bailey snoozed in his dog bed.

"Did you take care of her?" my mother asked.

Take care of sounded a little ominous. But it was hard not to read too much into things where my parents were concerned.

"I convinced her not to call the vet." Knowing I wouldn't get any thanks from my parents, I didn't wait for any. I opened my planner on the table and glanced at the wall clock. "Now, we've got a hike scheduled—"

"I'm not really feeling it." My father stretched. "I'd rather relax at the B&B."

"I read your Bigfoot investigation protocol last night." My mother lowered her chin to look at me. "It's a little woolly, no pun intended."

My insides hardened. Did I do *anything* right in her eyes? "That booklet is just for fun."

She sniffed. "With all the training we gave you, I'd think you'd be a bit more up-to-snuff on surveillance techniques."

I'd blocked most of those techniques from my mind. *Intentionally.* "You wouldn't want me to give away trade secrets, would you?" I gritted out.

"True," my father said. "Best keep it vague."

"Well..." I studied my planner. If they didn't want to hike, I had other things to do. "Then I've got an errand to run."

"Murder investigation?" my mother asked.

Reluctantly, I nodded.

"I'll come with you," my mother said. "Your father may be sleepy, but I'm not."

I commanded myself not to scream. "Oh," I said. "Good."

·❤· ·❤· ·❤·❤·❤·

My mother eyed the door to the spice shop. "Excellent. I wanted a refill on that coconut-lime white balsamic." She marched inside the small wooden building, in a charming brick alley behind Main Street.

More slowly, I followed. She and my father had had an "incident" inside the shop over a year ago. I really hoped the owner didn't remember.

Derek Anderson, spice shop owner and Sophie's ex-boyfriend, looked up from behind the high wooden counter. His welcoming smile faltered, and he pressed his hands to his graying head.

My chest grew heavy. He remembered all right.

I cleared my throat and strode through the maze of round tables displaying salt, cutting boards, cheese knives, and jars of spices and dry rubs. At the counter, I craned my neck at him. He was nearly as tall as Arsen. "Hi, Derek. How was your weekend?"

"Okay." He rubbed his thickening middle and studied my mother. She plucked a green bottle from a shelf and studied the label. "Have we met?" he called to her.

"Only briefly." She grabbed a second bottle and brought them to the counter. "A very rude man struck me with his cane, and my husband took offense. It was ages ago. I'm surprised you remember," she said in a pleased tone. "It's a sign of a clear mind."

Looking uncertain, he swallowed and turned back to me. "What brings you here, Susan?"

"My mother wanted some balsamic—"

"She's your mother?" he yelped.

"And I wanted to extend my condolences on Sophie's death," I finished.

He blinked then dropped his head. "Oh. Sophie. What a waste. I read about it in the paper."

"Did she, er, contact you at all?" I asked. "Let you know she was coming?"

"No," he said. "I wish she had. I mean, it was over between us long ago. I'm married with kids. But it would have been nice to see her again. She was a good person, a lovely woman."

"What do you know about her death?" my mother asked, tone hard, and I frowned. That wasn't the right approach in a murder inquiry. Besides, this was *Derek*. Whoever heard of a killer named Derek?

He blinked more rapidly. "What do I...? I don't know anything, just what I read in the papers."

"Obviously, whoever killed her was a part of her past here in Doyle," my mother said. "*You* were a part of her past in Doyle."

"That's not—" he sputtered. "I'm not— What are you accusing me of?"

"That much should be obvious," she said. "I'm accusing you of murder. I'm surprised the police haven't been to see you yet."

My jaw tightened. "Mom, why don't you wait outside? I need to buy..." My gaze landed on a pink salt cutting board. "A cutting board."

She shrugged. "I'll be outside." Her gaze narrowed. "But if you're not out in five minutes, I'm coming in."

"I'll get the board." Derek zipped around the counter and grabbed the largest. My mother ambled from the shop.

"I'm sorry about that," I said. "My mother thinks she's a detective."

He laughed uneasily. "Don't worry. I get it. My mother thinks she's still twenty-eight. It's embarrassing. You should see the clothes she wears."

He rang up the board. "Oh. I didn't even ask if this was the board you wanted? There are smaller ones that are less expensive."

"It's fine." *Anything to make up for my mother.* "My mother's been a little crazy about this murder. If you remembered anything about Sophie, it'd get her off my back."

"Remember?" He ripped tissue paper off a roll on the counter and set the cutting board in the center.

"Any little detail about Sophie would help."

"A detail?" He smiled. "Sophie didn't drive. Driving terrified her. I used to drive her and young Arsen down to Angels Camp to visit his aunts. They're great ladies."

Scratch that. Not *everything* was helpful. "What about the days after the Holidays' car accident? Was Sophie acting worried or concerned? Did she say anything to you?"

"Worried? She was a wreck. She loved that couple and their son. Sophie was brokenhearted after the accident. She blamed herself."

I rubbed my cheek. The aunts had said something similar. Resting my hand on the high counter, I leaned closer. "Why would she blame herself?"

"I think Sophie thought she should have stopped them. But she didn't even realize they'd left."

"Was that usual? For the Holidays to leave Arsen without telling her they were going?"

Derek frowned. "No, I don't think it was. I think... She thought she'd upset them somehow. She worried that's why they hadn't stopped by to let her know they were going out."

"How would Sophie have upset them?"

The big man blew out his breath. "It was stupid. Mrs. Holiday thought someone had been in her bedroom. She said there were some articles of, er, clothing missing."

My breath hitched. Had he put a slight emphasis on the word *said*? "You mean lingerie?"

"The maid probably wrecked it in the laundry and didn't want to fess up to it." He taped the tissue paper around the salt board. "It was nothing."

"And Mrs. Holiday accused Sophie?" *Eeesh.* That would be awkward.

"Not accused. Asked her about it. Sophie denied it, but she worried Mrs. Holiday didn't believe her."

"And when was this?" I asked.

"Not long before the accident. Sophie thought they'd fire her, but they didn't. Then the accident happened, and she had to leave anyway."

"It sounds like you don't quite believe the story. Not that Mrs. Holiday didn't accuse Sophie of going into her room, but that Mrs. Holiday wasn't being honest."

He slid the board into a brown paper bag. "I went over to the house one night to pick Sophie up. When Mrs. Holiday saw me getting out of my junker in her driveway, she went ballistic. She acted like I'd come to rob the place. Then Sophie came flying down the stairs to explain, and she backed off. But I could tell she wasn't happy. Mrs. Holiday was what they called high-strung. Today we'd just call her unstable, maybe a personality disorder of some kind. I never believed that so-called accident was a murder-suicide."

I drew back from the counter. "What do you mean?"

"I mean Mr. Holiday wasn't the murderer. He was the victim."

Chapter 14

I HADN'T BELIEVED THERE could be anything worse than thinking your father had murdered your mother. But believing your mother had been mentally unstable, that *she* may have killed your father... *Was that worse?*

I didn't know. And I didn't know if that's what had happened. After all, the owner of the spice shop had been guessing. It had been an educated guess, but it was still a guess.

And I was rationalizing not telling Arsen what I'd learned. It wasn't the best way to start a marriage.

Feeling slightly sick, I left the spice shop, reemerging in the brick alley. My mother leaned against the picnic table and pretended to read a local paper. She folded it, pages rustling, and tucked it beneath one arm. "Learn anything?"

"Mrs. Holiday accused Sophie of stealing. It happened not long before the accident." I'd just stick to the facts. If Arsen's mother had had mental challenges, the aunts would know. But would they admit it?

"Hm." She checked her watch. "We need to collect your wedding dress."

Which would give me the perfect opportunity to question the aunts. But I couldn't do it with my mother hanging around. I shook myself. I'd figure out something. We walked back toward my blue car, parked on the street.

"I suppose you're wondering how I managed to dislodge your bodyguard, Ghost, today?" she asked.

"Did you drug him too?" I asked tartly.

"Of course not. I told him I'd watch you, and that Dixie needed help with a leaky rivet in her trailer."

I winced at the plastic sheet covering my Crosstrek's rear window. "Does she?"

My mother shrugged and opened her car door. "It's a common problem with trailers like hers. And there are things we need to discuss before the wedding."

"I told you, we can't do anything about that rooster." I slid inside the SUV.

"I'm not talking about your neighbor's bird. This is about you. When a woman gets married, things change." She snapped her seatbelt on. "And a little preparation goes a long way."

"Preparation for what?"

"I'm talking about protection."

Heat flooded my face. *This* was the talk we were having? She must have guessed that Arsen and I by now had...

Hadn't she? I started the car and pulled from the curb. "It's fine. We're fine," I choked out. *Radical honesty. Be honest.*

"It's important to manage expectations. Or specifically, to ensure that both partners have similar expectations. The first time is always more difficult for the woman."

"Mom, it's... We... It's not our first time," I blurted.

"What?" She reached across the seat and grasped my thigh. "Oh, Susan. I'm so sorry."

I squirmed in my seat. "There's nothing to be sorry about. It was fine. Great, really."

My mother drew away. "I don't think you need to take *that* tone. Your enthusiasm's frankly disturbing."

I risked a glance at her. "Are you telling me you and Dad don't, ah... Enjoy it?"

"We do take pride in a job well done, but that's not to say we *enjoy* it."

My hands tightened on the wheel. Now I was disturbed. This was way too much information about my parents' private lives.

She sighed and rummaged in her purse. "Oh, well. I'd hoped this would be more of a delightful surprise for you. But it is what it is. No one knows the joy of waiting anymore. Anticipation is so underrated these days."

She pulled a small white box from her purse and opened it, exposing a froth of white lace and garters. "Your thigh holster. I thought you could wear it under your wedding gown."

I blinked. "Wait. What? What are we talking about?"

"My gun is back at the house," she said. "It's the ideal size for concealed carry. But I guess you already know all about that. If you had to kill someone, I don't know why you didn't talk to me about it. I'm your *mother*. Taking a life takes a psychological toll."

"I haven't killed anyone!"

"Then what were you talking about?"

"What were *you* talking about?"

"Arsen knows how to handle himself. He was a Navy SEAL after all. But I didn't think you'd kept up with your training. And you were rather hopeless as a child."

My brain adjusted to this new information. "You wanted to talk to me about protecting myself with a gun," I said slowly. "Before the wedding."

"I'd planned to give you my favorite mini semi-automatic as a wedding gift. But with everything that's been going on... Well, you *do* tend to get yourself into trouble. What did you think I was talking to you about?"

My face grew hotter. "Never mind," I muttered.

"The thigh holster is a set, see? There are holsters in white, ivory, and black lace plus matching garters. Much more convenient than storing your gun in a purse."

"They're lovely," I choked out.

"Trust me," she said. "Arsen will love them."

"Let's talk about something else," I said wildly.

She laughed. "Oh, Susan. Don't be such a prude. You're getting married!"

My mother needled me with ribald wedding-night talk all the way to the aunts' mansion. We pulled into the driveway. I speed-walked to the tall front door, leaving my mother behind.

The door stood open, which seemed a little lackadaisical, considering. I barreled inside the wide, modern hallway, and collided with Junior.

His shark-like eyes narrowed. "Careful." With his meaty hands, he brushed off the front of his golf shirt as if I'd left cooties behind.

"Sorry," I said. "Are you going out?" A car door slammed behind me.

"Not that it's any of your business, but yes."

"Junior, I'm sorry for all the bad blood between your family and Arsen's. We would love to patch things up and just be family again."

His tanned face wrinkled in a scowl. "It's too late for that. Not that it matters anymore."

"Obviously, it does matter." To him, at least. And family was important to Arsen.

Junior smiled thinly. "Don't feel bad. This trip has changed everything, if not the way you hoped. I'll get what I deserve." He jerked his head toward the wide, modern stairs. "The aunts are upstairs.

There's some drama going on, but I'm out." He strode past me and outside.

My mother joined me in the hallway. She watched Junior's departing bulk. "That one's trouble, mark my words."

"The aunts are upstairs," I muttered, uneasy. What sort of drama was going on? Weddings tended to be fraught with problems. But the point of planning was to avoid them. And I'd planned to the hilt.

"Let's get that dress." My mother climbed the floating stairs, her fingers grazing the black metal railing.

I hurried after her. At least no one else was dead. Junior could be a pain, but not even he would call murder a *drama*.

A feminine shout rang down the hallway, and my stomach spasmed. My mother and I met each other's gaze. We strode toward the action.

Anabelle emerged from a doorway and stopped short. Her eyes widened. "Oh!" Her gray hair was wilder than usual, as if she'd tugged it into anxious tufts. A yellow silk scarf trailed low down her back. It threatened to slip off the shoulder of her red top.

Anabelle clapped her plump hands to her mouth. "Oh, Susan. I'm so sorry. I don't know how this happened."

"What's happened?" my mother asked, brisk.

She gulped. "It's terrible. Just terrible. But you're such a good planner. You have a backup, right?"

"A backup what?" I asked, growing cold.

"A backup... dress?" she whispered.

My muscles relaxed. Was that all? "For the rehearsal dinner? That's not a problem." I didn't care what I wore for that. We were all friends and family, and I had several appropriate outfits.

"No," Anabelle said. "For the wedding." She pivoted and hurried into the room.

I stared, unmoving. My mouth went dry. *For the...?* I'd misheard. She couldn't have meant the wedding dress.

My mother grasped my arm and shook it. "Susan? Susan!"

"I'm fine." This had to be a misunderstanding. I strode into a guest bedroom with a high, beamed ceiling. Watercolors of mountain landscapes decorated the white walls.

Judith straightened away from the bed in the center of the room. Her expression was grim. "Susan." She shook her head and looked away.

My wedding dress lay atop the white coverlet, and I breathed a sigh of relief. It was fine. I stepped toward it, my hand outstretched, and I stopped, swaying, as if I'd run into a cold, hard wall.

The dress wasn't fine. It had only seemed that way against the white bedspread. Long gashes ripped the bodice and skirt.

My beautiful wedding gown—the gown Arsen's mother had worn—was ruined.

Chapter 15

THE GOWN. MY LEGS folded beneath me. My mother caught my arm. She led me to the long, leather seat at the end of the bed.

Whoever had destroyed my wedding dress hadn't thoughtfully slashed it along its seams. They'd attacked it in a frenzy. Bits of down from the comforter lay in tufts, where the coverlet too had been slashed. The mattress must have been damaged as well in the attack.

But the mattress and comforter could be replaced. The gown couldn't. There was no way to repair it. It was done, reduced to rags. I swayed, sickened, on the tan-leather seat.

"I'm so sorry," Anabelle whispered. Her round face crumpled.

Judith shook her head. "Nonsense. How could you have anticipated something like this?"

First the murder, then the favors, and now the gown? *All my wedding plans.* I stared, uncomprehending, at the gown laid out on the bed and burst into tears.

I couldn't help it. It was too much. I had a deluxe, top-of-the-line leather-bound wedding planner. And I hadn't planned for *any* of these disasters. And yes, I *know* the murder was the worst. But my gown!

"It's only a dress," my mother said.

"Only a dress?" I gasped. "It belonged to Arsen's mother. It had history. It fit me perfectly. I designed our rustic wedding theme around that dress. The baby's breath and pink rose centerpieces were reminiscent of the lace. I *loved* that dress." How was I supposed to pull off the wedding now?

"You loved it more than you love Arsen?" my mother asked.

I drew myself up. "Of course not," I snapped. "How can you say...?" I trailed off.

My mother arched a brow.

I swallowed, hating that she knew how to snap me out of near-hysterics better than nearly anyone. And I did need to snap out of it. Wailing and gnashing my teeth wasn't going to fix this.

"I'm sure I'll be able to find another white dress." Shopping would cut into my other plans for the week, but I'd find *something*. And there was always the internet.

Anabelle cleared her throat. "I always thought it was a bit odd when the bride looked too much like the wedding cake. The guests *eat* the cake."

"The symbolism is definitely strange," her sister agreed.

I shook myself and pulled my everyday planner from my purse. My throat hardened. I flipped to the criminal investigation section. I'd worry about finding a new dress later. Now I had to focus on something else before I started crying again.

"What happened?" Pulling my pen from its sleeve, I held it poised above the page.

"I don't know," Judith said. "We came up here ten minutes ago and saw this." She motioned toward the bed.

"When was the last time you saw the dress intact?" I asked.

"When we laid it out," Anabelle said.

"What time was that?" my mother asked.

"Around one o'clock this afternoon, I think," Anabelle said.

"One-oh-five." Judith clawed a hand through her close-cropped gray hair. "I checked my watch as we were leaving the room. We were late for lunch."

"And then you and the guests left the house for lunch?" I scribbled notes on my planner page.

"No," Judith said. "We had lunch here. Everyone seemed to want to relax and lounge at the house."

"And by everyone, you mean Louis, Nanette, and Junior?" I asked.

My mother cut her gaze to me. Her expression was inscrutable. I shifted my weight.

"Of course," Anabelle said. "Why?"

Judith's mouth tightened. "Because one of them most likely did this. Just as one of them most likely killed poor Sophie."

"Oh, no," Anabelle said. "I can't believe that. It must have been, er, someone else," she faltered.

"Where are Louis and Nanette now?" my mother asked.

"We left them in the bar," Judith said.

"Hmph." My mother pivoted on her sensible heels and strode from the bedroom.

I leapt from my chair and hurried after her. My mother had been a terrific spy. But her interrogation methods could be a little rough.

"Mom," I said as we trotted down the stairs. "Let me handle this."

"Nonsense. You've got a new dress to acquire. I'll take care of the suspect interviews."

My pulse skittered. "No, really. It's fine."

She turned a corner and walked down a long hallway to a bar. It was empty. She jammed her hands on her hips. "Drat it. Why does this house need *two* bars?"

"Honestly, I don't think—"

She brushed past me. "It's unnecessarily ostentatious. But I suppose I'll have to get used to it."

"Why?" I asked, trailing behind her.

She marched back down the long hall. "Because you and Arsen will be moving in after the wedding."

My head jerked back as if I'd been slapped. "What? No. Why would we move in with Anabelle and Judith?"

"Not *with* them. They'd move out, of course."

"We're planning on living at Wits' End," I said. "I have to be there to manage the B&B. Why would you think we were taking over the mansion?"

"Because Judith told me you would. She said it was understood that Arsen would move into the family home once he married. The house belonged to his parents, after all."

"Well, I don't know where she got that idea, but—" We rounded a corner and walked into the lounge area. Louis and Nanette relaxed with goblets of red wine in front of a massive stone fireplace.

Nanette twisted in her leather chair and smiled. "Was the final fitting a success?" Her elegant ivory silk blouse and matching slacks skimmed her slender frame.

"Not exactly," I said.

"There's been an incident." My mother went to stand with her back to the fireplace. Her legs were slightly apart, her arms seemingly relaxed at her sides.

Louis's patrician brows lifted. "An incident?" His collar was open, and he wore navy slacks and boat shoes.

"Someone slashed the wedding dress," my mother said. "It's ruined."

Nanette gaped. "That's... What?"

"Where were you between one and five o'clock this afternoon?" my mother asked.

Carefully, Nanette set her wine goblet on a polished wooden end table. "You're accusing us?" she asked, voice taut.

"We're hoping you may have seen someone or something," I said quickly. But *someone* in this house had done it.

Louis sipped his wine. Furrows appeared between his blue-gray eyes. "But it had to have been one of us. I never liked the idea that a random vagrant or psychopath stumbled across Sophie. It didn't make sense. Not in this place."

He motioned with his glass to the windows overlooking the golf course. The sky above the emerald grass had turned a deeper shade of blue, signaling the coming twilight.

Nanette frowned. "The only people I saw here were us." She nodded toward Louis. "Well, you and Judith and Anabelle. Junior spent the day skulking in his room."

Louis sighed and set his glass beside Nanette's on the low table. "He would be a much happier man if he'd let his childhood resentments go."

"And you were together the entire time?" my mother asked. The fire popped.

"No, of course not," Nanette said. "But if you want me to account for everyone's comings and goings, you're out of luck. I didn't think I had to pay attention. Is the gown really ruined?"

"It's a total loss," my mother said. "There's no way to salvage it except as a rag."

A pang of rage and regret choked my throat. Yes, I was going to be an adult about this. It *was* only a dress. But my brain and my heart had two different opinions on the matter.

"Who could have done such a thing?" Nanette asked.

"Do you really have to ask?" Louis said. "Junior's been griping about this wedding ever since he arrived. He hates all this. It reminds him of everything he thinks he should have."

"He's been behaving like an ass," she admitted. "But I don't think his anger is aimed at Susan. And to destroy her dress like that..." She shook her head. "Why?"

A worm burrowed deep into my gut. Nanette had a point. Attacking the dress did seem personal. And very, very disturbing.

"What are you going to do?" Nanette asked me.

I forced a smile. "Carry on, of course. After all, it's only a dress. I'll get a new one."

Arsen and Ghost ambled into the room, and my stomach plunged. *His mother's beautiful dress.* How was I going to tell him?

"New dress?" Arsen asked. "What's wrong with my mom's?"

Chapter 16

FRUSTRATED, I SLID THE cocktail dress back onto its rack. I'd hoped to find a simple white dress at one of the boutiques in Doyle this morning. It was June after all, and lighter, summer colors were popular. But I wasn't having any luck.

"Don't like it?" Arsen asked. He was wearing his usual security company uniform of navy golf shirt and khakis. I hoped that meant he'd been too lazy to find a different shirt and not that he had to run to Sacramento again.

"It's not right for a wedding," I said.

He rubbed my back. "Hey, I don't care what you're wearing, as long as you're at the altar."

I turned and leaned against his chest. "I'm so sorry about your mother's dress."

"It's only a dress," he said, gruff, and held me tight. "But I'm not letting you out of my sight again. I don't care if seeing the dress before the wedding's bad luck."

I didn't see how our luck could get much worse. "Maybe I'll find something online." There was always expedited shipping.

"We could go to Sacramento and look. Or even to San Francisco."

I looked up into his handsome face. His hazel eyes were somber. "I don't want to take that much time away from our guests," I said.

Especially since one of them was a killer. My chest hardened. One of our *guests* had ruined that gown.

Or Judith or Anabelle had done it, and I didn't even want to think that. I swallowed. "Arsen, I heard there's some understanding that we'll move into the mansion."

He laughed, releasing his hold on me. "It's not a mansion."

I stepped back. "Fifteen-thousand square feet *is* a mansion, but that's not the point. Why do people seem to think we're moving in?"

"It was always assumed growing up that I'd take over the place when I got married." He braced his elbow on the dress rack, and it wobbled. "But you've got Wits' End. Nothing's changed. We'll live at the B&B."

"Are you sure you want to?" I asked, worried. "It's less modern and a lot smaller than you're used to."

"In Afghanistan I shared a shipping container with three guys for six months. Don't worry about small. And my aunts' house is too big for the two of us."

And when we had kids, Wits' End would soon be too small. Staying at my house had seemed so obvious when we'd talked it over months ago. Now I wasn't so sure. I gnawed my bottom lip. I wasn't sure about much at all anymore.

We returned to my B&B. As we entered the high-ceilinged foyer, voices emerged from the Victorian's kitchen. We glanced at each other and hurried across the Persian carpet. Arsen pushed open the kitchen's swinging door.

"Roswell was obviously a cover-up," Dixie was saying. "The question is what were they covering up? Military tech or aliens?"

"Or military tech that was reverse engineered from alien technology," Ghost said.

"I did know this retired Air Force dude—" Dixie looked up from the small table and noticed us. "Any luck?" she asked me.

"None," I said. "I'm going to try online."

Ghost lounged against the butcher block counter, a coffee mug in his hand. "How can we help?"

"Keep an eye on Dixie," Arsen said.

My cousin straightened in her chair. "What? Why? I don't need to be watched." In his dog bed beneath the table, Bailey looked up, alarmed.

"After the attack on the dress," Arsen said, "I'm not taking chances. Someone could be trying to stop the wedding, and you're both a part of that."

Ghost canted his head. "Why stop the wedding?"

Color crept up Arsen's cheeks. "My father, uh, had some ideas about maturity and marriage."

I stared at him. What sort of ideas? And why would they stop the wedding?

Ghost's olive brow wrinkled. "And?"

"My father's company transfers into my control after I get married."

My mouth fell open. "What? I thought... I mean..."

My pulse throbbed in my ears. I hadn't really given Arsen's finances much thought. I'd assumed everything would keep on going as it always had. He'd always had money, and his parents' company had run fine without his input.

But if he took control of the chip company... That changed everything.

My brain scrambled to make sense of it all. "What about your security firm?" I asked.

"Nothing's going to change," Arsen said. "I'll have to attend board meetings, but Nanette's going to stay in charge. We've talked it over. I'm not a tech guy. It doesn't make sense for me to be running things there."

"Does Nanette know?" I asked.

"Of course."

"Why didn't you tell me this before?" I asked. We were getting married. And though we weren't getting married for financial reasons, finances were still important. I had an entire section in my planner devoted to budgeting.

Arsen shrugged. "Like I said, nothing's going to change."

"But you think it might be a motive for murder? Obviously *something's* going to change," I said hotly. This was huge. What else was he keeping from me? "No wonder people think we're moving into the mansion."

"Whoa." Dixie leaned back in her kitchen chair. "What?"

"I told my aunts I'm staying at Wits' End," Arsen said.

"They didn't seem to believe you," I said.

"They're keeping things open."

I narrowed my eyes. "Open?"

Arsen grimaced. "They think I may change my mind later. And who knows? Maybe someday we will."

"So what you're telling me is, by marrying me, you're coming into a ton of money."

Ghost straightened off the counter. "I'm just going to, uh..." He strode to the porch door and outside. Bailey trotted behind him, the beagle squeezing out the door before it could completely close.

"Yeah, me too." Dixie followed them onto the porch.

"No," Arsen said. "The money, the company, were always mine. I'm technically coming into control of it now. But like I said, I don't know anything about running chip companies. Nothing changes. My finances are the same. I just have more responsibility."

"Why didn't you say anything about this before?"

"Why does it matter?" he asked in an exasperated tone.

"I don't know. Maybe it doesn't. But it seems kind of important. And if we're getting married, shouldn't we share these things?"

"If?" His square jaw hardened.

I exhaled heavily. "Of course we're getting married. But if we're going to have a strong marriage, a happy one, we can't be surprising each other with these *oh-by-the-ways*."

Arsen looked at his hiking boots. "You're right," he said in a low voice. "I'm sorry. I'm not used to..." He looked up, and his gaze met mine. "I think I've kind of been avoiding it in my own head. Maybe I've been fooling myself, telling myself it didn't matter, that nothing would change. I don't..."

He shook his head. "The company my parents built isn't my world. It never was. I'm not comfortable in it. I feel like I'm in over my head. I don't want to mess things up. Thousands of people work there. Their livelihoods depend on that company. For me to come in could cause problems."

My pulse slowed. I took his hand. And this *wasn't* the old, irresponsible Arsen returning. Quite the opposite. He was worried about doing the right thing. "You're not going to mess things up."

He laughed hollowly. "Running a one-man security consulting firm is a lot different than managing an international, multi-billion-dollar corporation."

Billion-dollar? I held his hand a little tighter to steady myself. No wonder Junior was still bitter.

"And it's not the kind of life we'd enjoy," he continued. "Nanette works eighty-hour weeks, at least. This is her first vacation in six years. I didn't want that for us. Do you really want to be married to a workaholic?"

No, I didn't. But first Arsen had given up a high-flying career and now a billion-dollar company for me. It was a lot. I tried to swallow. Would he come to regret it? To regret me?

I raised my chin. Whatever Arsen was, he wasn't weak. And I wasn't going to treat him as if he was. He knew his own mind, even if he did have doubts about his parents' company.

"But you know your limits," I said. "You know what you don't know. And Nanette is still there, like she's always been."

"And when she retires?"

"We find another Nanette," I said. "Or the board does. You're not on your own."

Arsen kissed my forehead. "I know." He pulled me close. We stood there for a long moment, and I listened to the steady thump of his heart. Then he sighed, and we broke apart. "Let's find you a new wedding dress."

We ended up finding three. Arsen insisted we order them all, in multiple sizes, just to make sure at least one of them fit. And while this may sound extravagant, the dresses weren't all that expensive. It's funny. Once you remove the word "wedding" from "wedding dress," long white gowns get a lot cheaper.

I finished in time to make it to lunch at the fifteen-thousand-square-foot-not-a-mansion. Arsen and I drove there with my parents, Dixie, and Ghost. The latter argued about the latest Pentagon UFO report through the entire ride.

But it was a friendly argument. Maybe Dixie was recovering from her Valentine's Day disaster with the so-called Steve. I drummed my fingers on the window frame. Had she ever figured out what the guy's real name was?

I shook my head. *Unlikely.* If she'd found out "Steve's" real identity, she'd have extracted revenge and been feeling *much* better by now.

Ghost seemed like a great guy to recover with from her heartache. Ideal, even. What were the odds Arsen's best man would be into UFOs too?

We found everyone on the paving stone patio overlooking the mountains. The aunts had hired a caterer. A small but elegant buffet had been set out beneath a white awning. The family, in bathing suits and cover-ups, mingled around the long table.

"Did you have any luck?" Nanette, in a striking two-piece and matching tropical sarong, ambled toward us.

"I think I've found a dress." I wrapped an arm around Arsen's waist. "It should arrive tomorrow."

She smiled. "What a relief. I'm so glad."

"You'll look lovely in whatever you find." Louis, his shirt open over his swim trunks, took a sip from his champagne flute. He looked around. "I see Junior's back to avoiding everyone. Or do you think he doesn't know lunch is being served?"

"I'll get him," Arsen said grimly. "It's time Junior and I had a real talk." He kissed me and strode across the patio and into the house.

"I'm impressed with how well you've managed these trials," Louis said. "You really do have something of Arsen's mother in you."

High-strung? I shifted uneasily.

"She was unflappable," the lawyer continued.

"I'm extremely flappable." I frowned. Was that word? And why did people see Arsen's mother so differently? Derek Anderson had said she was high strung. Unflappable was the opposite of that. Had she simply been complicated?

I shook myself. "I'd prepared quite a bit for the wedding though. That's made it all easier."

"I'm surprised you didn't want to hold the wedding here." He motioned toward the rolling expanse of lawn.

The estate *was* spectacular, but my heart was at Wits' End. And suddenly the lunch looked a lot less appetizing. I'd been the one pushing for a Wits' End wedding, not Arsen. Would he have preferred to hold it here?

"We wanted to hold the ceremony in the B&B gazebo," I said lamely. "And the barn we rented seemed perfect for our rustic-themed reception."

But if we'd chosen the mansion, we could have held everything here—wedding and reception. It would have been more convenient for the guests. True, Arsen's parents had been married in the same barn Arsen and I had chosen for the reception. But maybe we were overdoing the nostalgia.

My glance darted toward the mansion Arsen had disappeared into. Having the wedding here would also have made Arsen's aunts happy. They had, in fact, suggested it.

"You're a romantic," the lawyer said.

My smile was tight. So romantic I hadn't given enough consideration to what Arsen wanted. My head had been too full of plans for *my* dream wedding.

I rocked slightly on the paving stones. This beautiful house, the jobs he'd given up for me. It was so much. *Would* Arsen come to resent it some day? "You may be right," I said in a low tone.

Louis took my hand and bowed over it, kissing it lightly. "Then you and Arsen will be perfect together." His hand lingered, warm and comforting on mine, and then he released me. "And I'm sure the wedding will be perfect too."

Anabelle fluttered over to us. "Eat, eat. We have all your favorites." She steered me toward the table laden with food and flowers. I loaded up a china plate.

Arsen strode across the patio to me, his expression taut. "Susan, I need you for a minute." He drew me away from the others to the edge of the pool.

"How did it go with Junior?" I asked.

"It didn't. He's dead."

Chapter 17

I CLUTCHED ARSEN'S ARM. *Junior? Dead?*

The sun sparkled off the swimming pool, its blue perfection reflecting the cloudless sky. Its surface rippled lazily, dreamlike. Behind us, the family murmured, cheerfully unaware.

Junior. This was awful. Bile clawed at my throat. "Oh, Arsen," I whispered. "Was it...?" *Murder?*

He nodded. "I've called the sheriff. She wants me to keep a lid on this until she gets here."

I glanced at my parents. They would be annoyed we'd kept them in the dark, but I could live with that. And they wouldn't be in the dark for long.

Five minutes later, sirens echoed off the mountains. My parents stiffened and glanced at each other. Dixie and Ghost did the same.

The others didn't react. Or they pretended not to. And I hated that I'd grown suspicious of them all, even innocent-looking Anabelle and forthright Judith.

"What happened?" I asked Arsen quietly.

He shook his head. "I found him in his bedroom. He'd been uh..." He glanced down at me, his expression troubled.

"What?"

He grimaced. "His throat had been cut. It was quick. But there was a lot of blood."

I pressed my hands to my mouth. "Arsen, Nanette knows how—"

Judith strode toward us. "Something's wrong. What is it?" she asked, brusque.

Arsen hesitated. "It's Junior. He's dead."

Judith's narrow face whitened beneath her tan. She swayed, and Arsen grasped her elbow to steady her.

"That's— How?" she croaked.

"The sheriff asked us not to discuss any details," he said. "She wants it kept quiet until she can arrive and manage the situation."

"How?" she demanded, her voice low and fierce.

"He was stabbed," Arsen hedged. "He bled out quickly."

That wasn't exactly what had happened. But I understood why Arsen was sugarcoating the news. No one wanted to hear a relative had died like that.

The sheriff and her deputies arrived. The section of the house with Junior's bedroom was cordoned off. Questions were asked. And though I should have done my best to eavesdrop on the interviews, I didn't have the stomach.

The sheriff had departed. But she'd left two men behind, still collecting evidence from Junior's room.

Arsen and his aunts and I had gathered in Judith's bedroom. We'd left my parents to their own devices.

Her bedroom was sparse, with a high ceiling and wood floors. Its windows overlooked part of the golf course. A set of clubs leaned in one corner.

I rested my head against Arsen's chest, his arms tight around me. "What do you want to do?" I asked him.

He looked down at me, his expression puzzled. "Do?"

"About the wedding," I said, and to my surprise, my voice was even. "We can postpone it."

"I don't care about the wedding," he said, and my heart sank.

I knew what he meant, of course. Two people had died, and a wedding was really... My throat clenched.

But it was our *wedding*. Heat built behind my eyelids. I hadn't planned on calling it off, but we could get married another time. This was a delay, not an ending.

"I'm marrying you on Saturday come hell or high water," he growled. "I don't give a damn if there's anyone there aside from a minister and witnesses."

"Oh," I said softly. I pressed my face to his chest so he wouldn't see the tears of relief that pricked my eyes.

"Unless..." he faltered. "Do you want to call it off?"

"No," I said quickly. "No, of course not." I stepped slightly away from him, and his arms loosened around me. "I want to marry you. I don't care about what dress I'm wearing or where it happens or who's there. I want to be with you."

His expression relaxed. "Good."

"But this is awful," I whispered and turned to Anabelle and Judith. "I'm so sorry for your loss."

On the edge of the bed, Anabelle blew her nose. "He was such a dear boy."

"Junior was a pill," her sister said sharply, turning from the picture window. Her shoulders crumpled inward, and she lowered her head. "But he didn't deserve to die."

"When did you see him last?" Arsen asked.

"He came down to breakfast at ten," Judith said.

"Junior finished the last of the bacon," Anabelle sobbed, her rounded shoulders quivering. "He loved that bacon."

"And then?" Arsen asked.

"He finished his breakfast and left," Judith said. "I presumed back to his room."

"There's something I need to tell you," Arsen said. "It looks like he was killed with your golf knife."

Judith's narrow face stilled. "What?"

"What's a golf knife?" I asked.

"In Judith's case," Arsen said, "it's a folding pocketknife. It's got a divot tool on one end and a built-in ball marker. The knife has a three-inch blade. It was lying open on the floor beside the body when I found him."

I only understood about half those words, but I nodded.

"I didn't—" Judith croaked. "You don't think I killed him?"

"Where did you keep your knife?" Arsen asked.

"There, when I wasn't using it." She motioned to the wooden bureau. "On top beside my loose change."

"Anyone could have taken it," I murmured.

"Did you do any golfing with the others?" Arsen asked.

Judith nodded. "We played yesterday afternoon." Her lips thinned. "I couldn't find my hybrid, but I used my knife quite a bit. Nanette admired it."

"Hybrid?" I asked.

"My new hybrid club," she said. "Hybrids are a cross between woods and irons."

"Does the sheriff know you're missing a club?" Arsen asked.

"No. Why should...?" Judith's lean face paled. "Sophie."

"What about Sophie?" Anabelle asked.

"The coroner thinks she may have been killed with a golf club." Arsen nodded toward the clubs in the corner. "You kept the clubs together in your room?"

"Yes," Judith said.

"What about the other guests?" I asked. "What were they doing between ten and noon, when Arsen found Junior?"

"Louis was swimming." Anabelle sniffed. "Not that he was in the pool the whole time. I went to join him at eleven, but he wasn't there. He returned to the pool a few minutes later, still wet. I think he'd gone to use the bathroom. Nanette joined us ten minutes later."

"Where was she before that?" I asked.

"I saw her coming out of her room around that time," Judith said. "She said she'd been catching up on some paperwork."

And the guest bedrooms were all in the same wing. My brow furrowed. I gazed out the window at the far-off sapphire lakes.

"There's something I should mention," I said. "Yesterday afternoon, my mother and I saw Junior leaving the mansion. He said this visit had changed everything for him, and he was going to get what he deserved. What did that mean?"

"I have no idea," Judith said.

"He did seem... happier," Anabelle said. "As if a weight had been lifted from his shoulders. I do hope he was happy at last."

"He seemed smug to me," Judith said.

"Any idea about what?" I asked.

Anabelle rose from the king bed and came to take my hands. "You wouldn't understand what a burden money can be. It was terrible for Junior. He always had plenty of money, but he always felt it wasn't enough, that he was lacking. Not like you."

I frowned. What was *that* supposed to mean? I wasn't lacking. I was on a budget, but everyone had a budget. Didn't they?

"He lived in a fantasy of being a deposed prince," Judith snapped. "His father gave up the company and was fairly compensated for it. It's not Arsen's fault or ours if his father squandered what he'd been given."

"It's not really Junior's fault either," Anabelle pointed out, releasing my hands.

"We all start out with certain advantages and disadvantages," Judith said. "It's up to us to make the best of them. Junior didn't. He was too sunk in self-pity and envy." She smiled at me. "That's what we always admired about you. You never complained about your lot. You just rolled up your sleeves and enjoyed what you had."

Uneasy, I glanced at Arsen, and he smiled faintly. "I'm pretty sure there's been *some* complaining," I said. Wits' End still needed a new roof. And my guests weren't always as charming as my B&B.

A saucer-shaped cloud floated above the tallest mountain peak. The cloud's shadow darkened the dots of pines.

"The point," Judith said, "is that Junior had plenty of advantages in life. Instead of building on them, he focused on what he didn't have. And he was a sneak and a liar."

"I wouldn't say that," Anabelle said.

"I would and I did," Judith said. "I saw him up here Sunday night outside Nanette's room."

"His room is just down the hall," Anabelle said. "Of course he'd be up here."

"Junior's room is by the stairs," her sister said. "He had no reason to come down this way. He was spying."

Arsen shifted his weight. "What do you think he was looking for?"

"Some company intel which would prove his father was cheated, no doubt," Judith said. "And of course he didn't find it, because it doesn't exist."

"And yet," Arsen said thoughtfully, "Junior was murdered."

"What are you saying?" Judith asked.

Arsen rested his hand on my shoulder. "I'm saying maybe Junior was right."

Chapter 18

ANABELLE STIFFENED BESIDE THE big bed. "Nonsense. No one cheated Junior's father. He panicked. The company was struggling. He wanted to take his money and run. And when he did, it caused serious problems for your parents. They had to borrow money to pay him out."

"And then he lost it all." Judith, backlit by the sun, turned from the picture window. The lines deepened on her craggy face.

"And that's when your parents' company took off," Anabelle said. "Of course, he wanted back in *then*. He tried to claim he'd been tricked, that pressure had been applied. But it was all nonsense."

"Where was Junior when Arsen's parents died?" I asked.

Anabelle's blue eyes widened. "Where?" She glanced at her sister. "He was with us at the old house. His father had gone off on some trip to Europe, and Junior was only eighteen. His father thought he should be with family."

"The old house?" I asked.

"In Angels Camp." She dropped onto the simple wood bench at the foot of Judith's bed. "It was a tiny little place. We were all bumping into each other and being very irritable. Of course, he'd just finished high school, so Junior was particularly surly. Youth, you know."

Angels Camp was only twenty minutes down the road. Junior would have had easy access to the mansion. But so would have Arsen's aunts. And I felt like a rotten betrayer for allowing the thought to even cross my mind. "Did he ever come to Doyle?" I asked.

"I suppose so," Anabelle said uncertainly.

"He did," Judith said. "Don't you remember? Sophie complained about it one day. Said he was lurking. She'd run into him somewhere on the estate, and it had startled her."

"Did she complain about anything else?" Arsen asked.

They glanced at each other again. "I don't know," Anabelle said. "It was all so long ago. She was quite distraught after the accident. And then when we realized she'd have to leave you... She cared very deeply for you, you know."

He sighed. "I can't remember any of that."

"Of course not," Judith said briskly. "Why would you? Now what do you want to do about all this? We can start calling the guests now and tell them the wedding's off."

Arsen took my hand. "Well?"

I swallowed. "I'm marrying you Saturday. If people want to come, they're welcome. If they don't, I'll understand. The only people I really want around me are already here."

He nodded. "Then the wedding's on."

Arsen and I sat at my kitchen table. I opened my laptop. The afternoon sun through the kitchen window whitened the computer screen, making it impossible to read. I shifted it on the table.

"Now's not the time for games of solitaire." My mother leaned against the butcherblock counter and sipped from a coffee mug.

"This is internet research," I said shortly. "On our suspects."

My father angled his head toward Arsen. "Don't you have better resources?" He stood beside my mother with a ham sandwich in his hand. We hadn't had a chance to eat after Junior's body had been found today.

Arsen nodded. "I've ordered up background checks on everyone. But we may as well see what we can find now."

"Everyone?" My mother arched a brow over her mug.

"Junior, Louis and Nanette," Arsen said.

"That's not exactly everyone," she murmured.

Muscles corded in his neck. "My aunts aren't suspects." Bailey looked up worriedly from beneath the kitchen table.

I laid my hand over Arsen's. "The sheriff won't think like we do. To her, everyone in that house is a suspect."

And either someone was trying very hard to make Judith look guilty, or she *was* guilty. But I couldn't believe she'd be stupid enough to use her own golf club and knife to commit a murder.

"Think like I do?" he asked. "You can't believe Anabelle or Judith had anything to do with these murders?"

"Of course not," I said. "But we should be thorough, if only to clear them from suspicion."

My mother looked through the blue-curtained window above the sink and didn't say anything. My father shook his head slightly.

My hands curled inward. Was I being dishonest? Everything I'd said was true. I *didn't* believe his aunts had anything to do with the murders.

But they'd both had means, motive, and opportunity. Judith could swing a mean golf club, and Sophie had been bludgeoned. And anyone could come up behind someone with a knife...

And both his aunts had benefited. After his parents' deaths, they'd moved into the mansion. They'd also gained access to a good deal of money. Had they misused it? Not that Arsen would have cared if they had.

"What did your aunts do before they came to take care of you?" my mother asked.

"School teachers," Arsen said tightly.

My parents exchanged looks. "Let's take a walk," my father said. "The afternoon's starting to cool off. I need some fresh air and exercise after everything that happened today."

"I do think better when I'm moving," my mother agreed.

The two walked out the door to the side porch. Their footsteps clattered lightly down the porch steps, and then there was silence.

I typed Louis Culshaw's name into the search engine. Dozens of articles popped up about the lawyer. I clicked the first.

Arsen cleared his throat. "Susan—"

The door from the foyer swung open hard. It banged against the wall, rattling objects inside their blue-painted cupboards. Beneath the table, the beagle started.

Dixie stormed into the kitchen, her chest heaving. "He... He..."

Arsen leapt to his feet. "What's wrong? What's happened?"

"He's a fraud!"

Ghost hurried into the kitchen after her. "Dixie, let me explain."

She whirled on him. "There's nothing to explain. He's *Steve*, the UFO jerk who ghosted me last February. And you've known who I was the whole time. This must have been hilarious for you. *Ghost*."

"It wasn't," he said, tone pleading.

She sneered. "You're more insidious than the Marxist indoctrination called Social Emotional Learning."

Ghost flinched. "But SEL came out of occult beliefs from the 1920s. It's warping kids' minds."

"*Exactly*."

Arsen leaned closer to me. "Social emotional...?"

I touched his arm. "We'll be homeschooling."

"So you had no idea who I was." Dixie crossed her arms over her olive tank top.

He shot Arsen a panicked glance. "I knew. I just didn't know how to tell you who I was. I felt terrible about February."

"Sure." She picked up my mother's discarded coffee mug and put it down again.

"Uh," Arsen said, "what's going on?"

"Steve," Dixie said hotly. "The guy who catfished me last February. Estevan is Steve."

Uh, oh. But Ghost was Arsen's friend, which meant he had to be a good guy. How could he have done that to Dixie? "But if he told you—"

"He didn't tell me," she said. "I saw it on his computer. He'd been in the UFO chatroom, and I saw his username."

"How'd you see his computer?" Arsen asked.

"I was in his room, obviously," Dixie said.

"Why?" I asked. We weren't cleaning the guest rooms again until after the wedding. Everyone was on their own.

Dixie glared. Arsen gave me a warning look. Ghost reddened.

Oh. My face warmed.

"You messed me around then," Dixie said. "And you've been messing around with me all week. You can forget about me helping with your best man's speech or with anything else." She slammed from the kitchen, her boots stomping down the porch steps.

"I should..." Ghost pointed toward the door.

"Go," Arsen said.

Ghost hurried after Dixie. The kitchen door banged shut behind him. Bailey snorted and sat on my foot.

I shook my head. "I don't think chasing after her is the right idea. She'll just dig in."

"Ghost can be persuasive."

"And Dixie can be stubborn."

Arsen's forehead crinkled. "There is that."

And I was focusing on Dixie's romantic woes because I didn't want to think about my own. *Were* we doing the right thing going forward with the wedding?

I returned my attention to the laptop and leaned closer to peer at the screen. My neck ached. Absently, I rubbed it. "Arsen?"

"Yes?" he asked, reading over my shoulder.

"I thought Louis Culshaw was the lawyer for your parents. I didn't know he was the lead counsel for their company."

He massaged my neck, and my hand dropped. "He sort of acted as both," he said. "He was always around for me, growing up. Not that I needed much legal help, but Judith and Anabelle occasionally did. They weren't just managing me. They were managing my money until I turned twenty-one. And they did a good job."

I tried not to groan with pleasure as his fingers kneaded my neck muscles. This was serious. "I know," I said. "They're wonderful women. You're lucky to have them in your life."

We nosed around the other articles on Louis. But I didn't find anything odd or suspicious. So I typed in Nanette's name. We scanned through more articles.

Nanette had been active on the social circuit. She'd turned up in the society pages almost as often as she appeared in the business pages.

I paused on a photo of her and Louis smiling at a black-tie dinner. Then I turned to the business articles. Most of the articles were admiring. But not all.

"She had some trouble with the board last year," I said neutrally.

"There was a takeover offer." His hand drifted down to work my shoulders. "It was a good one. Nanette convinced the board the company would be better off staying the course instead of selling. But it was a tough fight. The board was evenly split."

I tapped the round tabletop. "And in the middle of it, one of the board members died in a car accident."

"Frank," Arsen said heavily and released me. "He had three kids. All college age, but still. It was rough."

"How was he planning on voting?"

Arsen's jaw tightened. "He wanted to sell."

"I thought you weren't involved in the company." I studied him, my face warming. "It sounds like you know quite a bit about it though."

He shook his head. "I'm not involved. But selling the company was a big deal. Nanette kept me in the loop, since it would affect me."

"How? You would still have your shares, wouldn't you? I don't understand how it could have been sold without your agreement."

"I'm only a forty-nine percent stakeholder. The public owns the rest of the shares."

"When did the company go public?" I leaned back in my chair.

Arsen slung one arm over its back. "After my parents died, we came close to losing it again. Louis and Nanette took it public to raise funds. A fifty-one percent stake was sold. Judith and Anabelle agreed to it. The money was useful for me growing up."

I bet it was. "I'm sure the company's valued at a good deal more now."

He laughed shortly. "You could say that. I wish I hadn't brought it up."

"Brought up your ownership stake?" I asked.

"No, I mean a possible connection between the company and Sophie and Junior's murders. The more I think about it, the less likely it seems."

My brows drew together. Because I wasn't so sure it was unlikely at all.

Chapter 19

I TRIED TO SLEEP that night, but my mind kept going round and round about the wedding. I doubted Arsen's friends would be much fussed about the murders. They were all ex-military.

My friends were all from Doyle, so they knew what was happening. They could decide for themselves if they wanted to attend. I was fairly sure they would come though. A few stray cousins and uncles and aunts on my side would be driving here from the Bay Area. But I couldn't believe they'd be in any danger.

Still, were we doing the right thing?

When I finally fell asleep, I woke up an hour later to my neighbor's crowing rooster. My jaw ached. From grinding my teeth? I stared at my bedroom's dark ceiling.

Giving up on sleep, I threw off my covers and dressed. Dark moons hung beneath my eyes. It was *exactly* the sort of morale boost a girl needed pre-wedding. *Ha.*

I stumbled into my kitchen and made coffee. Outside the window over the sink, the yard had begun to lighten, the hillside glowing like fire.

I gazed into my full mug. Caffeine might wake me up, but it wouldn't do anything for my stress level.

I dumped my untouched coffee back in the pot and made breakfast for the family. I didn't really have to cook. But it was habit, and pottering around the kitchen was soothing.

Arsen ambled into the kitchen and kissed me. "Good morning, Beautiful."

"You're here early." I turned from the stove and ran my hand down his muscular arm. "Could you smell the bacon and pancakes all the way at your house?"

He laughed, pulling me close. "I thought you'd be up. Early rising's a hard habit to break."

I scowled. "Especially with the bantam menace next door."

"I'm surprised your parents haven't assassinated that rooster yet."

"They've tried," I said darkly.

He leaned a little away from me to get a better look at my face. "Are you serious?"

"There's been so much going on I haven't had a chance to tell you. My father attempted a black op. When the rooster fought back, they resorted to spiking the feed with sleeping pills. Unfortunately, all the chickens ate it. They're fine now, but Sarah came close to calling out the vet."

He laughed. "I didn't think your parents would be defeated by a bird."

Defeated? I doubted they'd given up. My stomach somersaulted. What would they try next? I pulled a flowered dishcloth from the stove handle and dried my damp hands.

"Are you okay?" Arsen rubbed my back, and I moaned with pleasure. "Wow, your muscles are tight," he said.

"I didn't sleep well last night," I admitted. And I had so many things to do today.

"Try not to worry," he said. "We'll figure this out."

How could I not worry? But I nodded. We *would* figure it out. But I didn't want anyone else to get hurt before we did.

Arsen helped me with the breakfast. We set up a table in the gazebo, and he carried out the chafing dishes full of food.

My parents and Ghost migrated from the Victorian to the gazebo, and we breakfasted there. The nearby UFO fountain splashed merrily. The gazebo's climbing roses and the pines on the hillside scented the air.

When we finished eating, no one was in the mood to move. We sat and drank mimosas. A measure of the tension in my shoulders eased.

Nanette rounded the corner of the Victorian and walked across the lawn toward us. She waved. "Something smells fabulous."

I nodded toward the table, laden with chafing dishes. "We've still got bacon and pancakes if you're hungry."

"I prefer not to get a massage on a full stomach," she said, climbing the gazebo steps.

"Massage?" I asked.

My mother smiled. "We thought it would be a surprise. Nanette and I are treating you and Dixie to a girl's spa day."

My stomach clenched. I couldn't go to a spa. I had to meet Jayce to collect the gift bags. Then I had to pack for the honeymoon, and—

"Where *is* Dixie?" Nanette looked around.

Ghost coughed and stood. "I've uh... Got to get a hike in this morning."

My father rose too. "I'll go with you. I can't let myself get soft in my retirement."

"You never mentioned what you retired from." Ghost descended the gazebo's white-painted steps.

"Accounting," my father lied, and the two men walked away. Nanette sat beside me.

My mother's coffee eyes narrowed. "Dixie is usually here for breakfast. And Ghost seemed uncomfortable when Nanette asked about your cousin. What's going on?"

"Dixie discovered that Ghost was the guy who, er, ghosted her last Valentine's Day." I grimaced. "Actually, she said he'd catfished her, but I think technically he ghosted her too."

"Ghosted?" My mother tilted her head back, emptying her glass of the last of her mimosa.

"Declined calls and stopped calling," I said. "It's a way to dump someone without actually saying it."

"How cowardly." My mother set her glass on the white-clothed table. "I would have thought a friend of Arsen's would have more backbone."

Personally, I'd *rather* be ghosted than told directly things weren't working out. Not by a long-term boyfriend, of course. That *would* be rude. But if I was just casually dating, that sort of rejection seemed easier to take.

"All may be fair in love and war," Nanette said. "But they take two very different types of courage. Shall we call Dixie? It sounds like she can use some pampering too."

I shook my head. "A spa's a lovely idea, but I've got so much to do—"

"Nonsense." My mother rose and smoothed her A-line skirt. "People put too much into weddings. It's only a party. Everyone will have fun because they love you and there's alcohol." Her brows lowered. "There will be alcohol, won't there?"

"Yes," I said hastily. "But I need to get the gift bags from Jayce, and—"

"We'll take care of that," Nanette said. "Now, let's get Dixie."

I called Dixie, and she agreed to meet us at the day spa. How a spa day was supposed to relax me when it hadn't been planned for was beyond me. But sometimes, you just have to try and go with the flow.

I collected my purse and jammed my planners inside. The three of us took my Crosstrek into downtown Doyle.

The spa was in a sky-blue craftsman with white trim off Main Street. Cheerful climbing flowers twined around the porch railing. A wooden sign of a sunflower hung from the eaves proclaiming DOYLE DAY SPA.

Nanette sighed. "It hasn't changed."

"You've been here before?" I asked, surprised.

She paused beside the blue-painted steps. "Arsen's mother lent the owner money to help with the down payment on this place. It wasn't much. An elderly aunt of Bergdis's had died and left her some funds. I confess, I'd hoped she'd invest it into our own business. But it was her money, and she wanted to put it into Doyle. And the owner paid her back within six months."

We stepped inside the foyer-turned-reception area. A woman with a silver streak in her titian hair greeted us from behind the high desk. "Welcome. You must be the Fortin party." She smoothed her gray smock.

A tortoiseshell cat sat on the desk, its tail coiled beneath him. The cat's whiskers twitched.

"I'm Nanette Fortin," she said.

"Is your cat friendly?" I asked reaching to pet its fur.

"No," the receptionist said, and I jerked my hand away. The cat growled. "And it's not ours," she continued. "It belongs to one of our neighbors, but we can't get it to leave. It goes where it wants."

Nanette laughed. "Typical cat."

"And you're booked for the Ultimate Pamper Package, I see." The receptionist gestured toward a natural-wood door. "This way to the changing rooms. Your friend has already arrived. She's in the salt relaxation room."

She led us to a changing area and gave us robes and slippers. We slipped into the seductively comfy robes. The three of us strolled to a room with soft lounge chairs and salt lamps on every end table.

Dixie, in a white waffle robe, peeled cucumbers off her eyes and looked up from her chair. "Oh. It's you." She returned the cucumbers to their places. A tray of cheese and crackers sat on the table next to the salt lamp. My cousin's feet rested in a copper bowl filled with water. Rose petals drifted on the surface.

The receptionist entered the room. She offered us a silver tray with fluted champagne glasses. "Mimosa?"

I'd already had one for breakfast, but what the heck? I was getting married in three days. "Thank you." Guiltily, I took a glass and sat beside Dixie.

"We only have two masseuses." The receptionist set a fresh tray of cheese and crackers on the other table between us. "So you'll be taking turns. Two will start with the scrub and massage. The others will have the hot oil scalp treatment and lavender sea salt foot scrub and foot clay masks."

Another woman entered the room and set a copper bowl at my feet. Gently, she removed my slippers and slipped my feet into the warm water. More bowls were set in front of Nanette and my mother, and the two spa employees left.

I sighed and wriggled my toes. "This is just what I needed. Thank you both. It's too bad Judith and Anabelle couldn't be here."

"I offered." Nanette nibbled a cracker. "But they said they don't like being touched by strangers."

"Completely understandable," my mother replied and sipped her mimosa.

Dixie grunted an assent. "Try the crackers."

After ten minutes or so, a woman led Dixie and my mother away for their massages. Nanette and I were taken to another room for our scalp treatments. Warm oil was massaged into our scalps. Lavender-scented dead sea salts were rubbed onto our feet.

The women slathered a white mask that smelled like oranges onto our feet with wide and slightly ticklish brushes. She wrapped our feet in warm towels, then departed.

Nanette sipped her mimosa. "Every time I get a spa treatment, I tell myself I'll do it once a month. I never do. Something always comes up."

"It's got to be hard to get away with all your responsibilities at the company. I can't believe you managed this whole week off for the wedding."

"It wasn't easy, but the responsibilities, the work, will be there when I get back." She smiled. "We need to pace ourselves."

"Does Louis?"

She arched a brow. "Louis? I suppose. You know how lawyers are. They work hard, play hard, and bill astronomically. He wasn't always that driven. But after Bergdis died—"

"Bergdis? Not John?"

Nanette glanced at me and smiled faintly. "Bergdis had a certain something. Everyone who met her fell in love. Louis wasn't any more immune than your father."

The tips of my ears warmed at the knowledge of this old secret. "Louis works full-time for the company, doesn't he?" I adjusted the warm towel on my head.

"Yes," she said. "Why?"

"Because it seems someone in that house is a murderer. I'd like to know who before anyone else gets killed."

The pipe music ended. Soothing instrumentals and whale calls drifted over the speakers.

She sighed. "And of course you think it must be me or Louis, because it can't be the aunts Arsen loves so well."

"I'd *rather* it be you or Louis," I said. "No offense."

She sipped her mimosa. "None taken."

"But if it were one of his aunts, it would be hard to take."

"I could tell you I didn't kill anyone, but I don't suppose my word would mean much to you. But..." She set down her champagne flute and met my gaze. "I will tell you that his aunts are not the sweet, innocent ladies-of-a-certain-age they appear to be."

My stomach rolled. "What do you mean?"

"I mean they get their way. Always, and no matter who may oppose them. Surely you've noticed that yourself?"

I frowned, and a trickle of oil ran down my temple and past my right eye. They did tend to arrange the world around them as they liked it. I'd never thought too much of it before. "That doesn't make them killers."

She raised a brow. "You don't know?"

"Know what?"

"Anabelle killed a man."

I stared. "What?" *What? Dithery Anabelle?* Judith seemed more likely to take such decisive and final action.

"It was before they came to take care of Arsen, back in Angels Camp. There was—"

An alarm rang shrilly, and we winced. The woman who'd wrapped my feet raced into the room, her eyes wide. "Fire. We have to get out. Now!"

Chapter 20

NANETTE JUMPED TO HER feet. "Which way?" she shouted over the blare of the alarm.

"Out the front," the spa worker said.

We shuffled down the hallway, the towels around our feet making us clumsy. Nanette swore and kicked one off.

It flew over her head and smacked me in the face. Gasping, I ripped the damp towel off me in time to see the second towel go flying. This time, I ducked, and it flew harmlessly past.

Shaking my own towels off my feet, I skidded on the hardwood floor, the mask slippery on my soles. I windmilled my arms like a cartoon coyote, then grabbed the walls for balance.

My breath accelerated. Where had I left my shoes? I should have at least kept the slippers they'd given me.

Hurrying after the spa worker, Nanette slid around the corner into the reception area. I followed. She tottered out the front door.

A low growl sounded behind me, and I turned. The tortoiseshell cat hunched behind a potted ficus tree in the corner. The cat hissed.

"Here kitty," I said nervously. "We've got to get out of here."

It growled and edged backward.

I grabbed it by the loose skin on the back of its neck and dragged it toward me. "Come on. We can do this." I lifted the cat to tuck it beneath one arm.

The animal howled and twisted, slashing at the sleeves of my robe. Streaks of pain scalded my arms.

"Ow!" I bolted onto the front porch. The cat launched itself from my arms. He raced between the small crowd standing in the front yard.

My mother, in her robe, hurried to me. "Thank goodness. I was about to go back in for you. That place is so old it's got to be a fire trap."

A siren wailed. I turned to look at the blue Craftsman. "I don't see any smoke," I said anxiously.

"That doesn't mean there's no fire," my mother said.

"Where's Dixie?" I asked.

"Here," she said from behind me. Dixie stood with her phone extended and aimed at me.

My eyes narrowed. A trickle of oil ran down the back of my neck. "What are you doing?"

"Filming for posterity."

Embarrassed, I touched the towel on my head. "Put that away. I look awful." I looked down. The once-white mask on my feet was flecked with dirt and grass from the yard.

Dixie smirked. "Why do you think I'm filming? Don't worry, we'll laugh about this later."

I very much doubted that. A fire truck screeched to a halt in front of the house. Men in canvas coats hopped from the truck and grabbed equipment. They hurried past us and inside the spa.

I studied my cousin. I hadn't had much time alone with her, and it didn't look like I'd get much chance with my mother around. This wasn't the ideal time, but I was on a schedule. I steeled myself. "Dixie, I talked to Gh—"

She glared.

"—Estevan," I amended. "He said the door to your trailer was open. He went in looking for you because he was worried."

Her mouth pinched. "And? What's your point?"

"Well, did you leave it open?"

"Maybe," she said. "But he's still a creep."

"But—"

A smaller, paramedic truck squealed to a halt behind the firetruck. A muscular paramedic with curling black hair stepped from the truck, and I flinched. It was Brayden Duarte, Jayce's husband. Face warming, I shrank away. I didn't want the town seeing me like this.

I edged through the crowd of women in front of the spa. If I could just get to my Crosstrek, parked on the street... My mouth tightened. I'd left my keys in the changing room with all my other things, like my phone. I couldn't escape.

A growl raised the hairs on my arms. I looked over my shoulder. The cat perched on the high fence between the spa and the house next door. Its shoulders hunched. I backed away and bumped into Nanette.

She frowned, then her face cleared. "I was worried when you weren't behind me. What happened?"

"The cat." I nodded toward the fence. And if I was stuck out in a yard, at least I could get more investigating done. The sheriff would expect no less. "Nanette, what did you mean, Anabelle killed a man? You were speaking metaphorically, right?"

"Ah, no." She adjusted the towel on her head. "She shot someone. Arsen's parents were terrified she'd be charged. You should ask Louis. He helped her out."

I frowned. "But... He's not a criminal attorney."

"Like I said, ask Louis." Her mouth compressed.

"But what—?"

"Why are you bleeding?" she asked.

"What?" I looked down. A thin rivulet of blood ran down my hand and dripped onto the lawn. Scarlet blossomed on the arm of the white robe.

"Paramedic!" Nanette called.

Brayden strode toward us. "Who's hurt?"

The tips of my ears grew hot. No, *no, no.* "I'm fine," I said hurriedly and made to leave.

"She's not," Nanette grasped my wrist and tugged up the sleeve of the robe. Long, bloody scratches ran from the inside of my elbow to my wrist.

I grimaced. "It's only a cat scratch."

"Those look deep," Brayden said. "They could get infected. Come with me." He led me to the back of his truck, sat me on the broad bumper, and cleaned and bound my arm. He smiled. "You'll be fine."

"I know." And soon the entire town would know about this too. I adjusted the collar of my robe and wished it was big enough to hide my head. "And thanks."

A man shouted his name. Brayden patted my arm. "Wait here." He strode toward the spa.

A coil of raspberry-scented smoke drifted past my face. "Up to more trouble, young Susan?"

Mrs. Steinberg walked around the corner of the red truck. Her cane thumped the pavement. Sun glinted off her black Jackie-O glasses. She stopped in front of me, her long, black dress swaying.

My mouth pinched. Was there anyone from Doyle who wasn't going to see me looking like I'd just crawled from an oil slick? "Not me," I said. "There's a fire." I nodded toward the Craftsman.

"No there isn't," she said. "It's a false alarm."

"How do you—?" Firefighters trooped from the house. "Oh," I finished. "Must be a faulty alarm," I said uncertainly.

She arched a white brow. "Do you really think so?"

I exhaled slowly. "No, I guess I don't." Pulling a fire alarm seemed immature, and it was a far cry from murder. Though slicing my dress to ribbons had seemed off too—more threatening than the alarm, definitely. But it had also felt childishly spiteful.

"What have you learned?" Mrs. Steinberg asked.

"Is it true that Anabelle shot someone?" I countered.

Mrs. Steinberg took a puff of her e-cigarette. "Yes."

"What happened?"

She shrugged. "It was Angels Camp and a long time ago."

"Angels Camp isn't that far away. It must have been big news here in Doyle, especially since Arsen's parents lived here."

"It was self-defense, and an amazing shot if I remember. But I'm a Doyle person. Wasn't my business."

"When was this?" I asked.

She tilted her head toward the blue sky. A thin stream of smoke shot from her mouth. "It was winter. I remember that. There was some business about footprints in the snow. It was the same year Arsen's parents died, but before the crash. Maybe January or February?"

"That's... a lot of death and disaster for one family." I pressed my hands to the front of my robe. Did Arsen know about this? He would have been too small to remember, and it was surely a painful memory for the women. I doubted they would have talked to him about it. But would he have heard from someone else?

"The man was in their house," she said. "They were two women alone. What was Anabelle supposed to do?"

"I don't know. I suppose... Could it be connected to what's happening now?"

She dropped the e-cig into the massive black handbag slung over her arm. "I don't see how."

"What did you mean about footprints in the snow?"

The lines on her forehead deepened. "I told you, I don't remember the details. It was a long time ago, and it wasn't Doyle." She angled her head toward the colorful spa. "It looks like you're wanted."

I glanced in that direction. My mother waved to me. "But—" I turned. Mrs. Steinberg had vanished. "How does she *do* that?" I muttered. Rising from the truck's wide bumper, I made my way to the ladies.

"A pulled alarm," Nanette fumed.

"I suppose everyone at the house knew we'd be here," I said casually. If there *was* more to this so-called prank than met the eye, my suspect list was limited. "I hope they haven't heard about the fire and are worrying."

Nanette shot me a sharp look. "Of course I told them where we'd be."

"I very much doubt the news has made it to the house yet," my mother said.

"It might have," Dixie said. "I posted my video online."

I scowled. *Seriously?* "Have you talked to Ghost? He's supposed to be escorting you to the reception." Okay, that was a little mean of me. But *honestly*. I didn't need a video of me looking like a greasy swamp creature online.

Her nostrils flared. "You mean *Steve?* No. That jerk can—"

"I'm so sorry," the titian-haired receptionist hurried toward us. "What a mess." She glanced down at my arm and sucked in her breath. "You've been hurt."

I raised my bloodied arm. "It was only the cat. You did warn me he wasn't friendly. Sorry about the robe."

She waved away my apology. "We'll get you a new one. And we'll give everyone an extra thirty minutes of massage. A teen must have snuck inside and pulled the alarm."

"Right," I said uneasily. "A teen." But had it been more than a silly prank?

Nanette tucked her arm inside my uninjured one and led me back up the porch steps and into the spa. "All right," she said. "I guess I'd better tell you the whole story."

Chapter 21

NANETTE AND I SETTLED into the spa room. Paintings with inspirational sayings decorated its distressed wood walls.

The spa workers managed to remove the mask, dirt, and grass from our feet. *And* they did it without making faces. They left us soaking our toes in copper baths.

"So," I said. "Anabelle."

Nanette sipped a fresh mimosa. "If you dig, I'm sure you'll find this in the papers. They reported a neighbor broke into their house, and Anabelle shot him in self-defense."

"They *reported*?" I asked carefully. "Are you saying they weren't honest?"

She shrugged. "He may have been Judith's obsessed ex-lover too."

"Too?" It was hard to imagine staid Judith inspiring obsession. But that wasn't fair. Obsession had nothing to do with the object and everything to do with the obsessed personality.

"After it happened, Arsen's father was understandably worried. It was obviously self-defense. The man who'd been shot was in his sisters' house, after all. But John didn't trust the local sheriff. He hired a private investigator to dig into things." She stared into her fluted glass.

"What did he find?" I asked, dreading the answer. What *had* that man been doing in their house?

"Nothing that the newspapers didn't. A spring had opened up on the dead man's property six months ago. The water was flowing into Judith and Anabelle's yard. There was some damage to their foundation, apparently. The sisters had tried to get the man to do something about it. But according to the law, since it was natural, it was up to them to divert the spring as they saw fit. This would have been costly, not to mention the damage already done to the foundation. When they finally sold their house, they took a major loss."

"That was when they moved to Doyle to take care of Arsen." Moving into the mansion must have been a godsend. But they'd have to have been insane to kill for the privilege. "And you think this is somehow connected to the recent murders?"

"I have no idea." She turned her head and met my gaze. "I'm simply saying that properly motivated, anyone can kill."

We finished our spa treatments. I rushed through changing into my street clothes and wandered through the spa. I finally found the fire alarm pull, in a short hallway by the back door.

I tested the door. It was unlocked. A teen *could* have snuck in and pulled it. My teeth clenched. But I didn't believe that was what had happened. Not for a minute.

A uniformed delivery man was trotting down Wits' End's front steps as we pulled into the gravel driveway. He waved and got inside his brown truck on the street, then drove away.

"Are you expecting a delivery?" my mother asked, stepping from the Crosstrek.

I frowned. "No—oh, the dresses." I hurried up the steps and through the screen door. Three wide, flat boxes lay stacked beside the B&B's front door. Hastily, I collected them and took them into the kitchen.

Bailey glanced up from his dog bed beneath the table. He snorted and flopped back down. I pulled a steak knife from the block and slid it beneath one of the box flaps.

"Whoa," Nanette said. "Careful with that. You may damage the dress, and that's no way to treat a steak knife. Allow me." She pulled a pocketknife from her slacks and flicked it open. Neatly, she slit the boxes.

Dixie opened them and peered inside. "Meh. The usual."

I pulled them out and studied them. The gowns were all lovely, but I gravitated toward the Grecian-style, off-the-shoulder gown. "What do you think?" I held it against my chest.

Nanette and my mother stared in horror. Dixie squinted. "Looks mythological. I like it."

"It's sleeveless," my mother said. "They all are."

"Well, yes," I said. "It's summer, and there's so much gown, sleeves seemed…" I looked down at the gown and my bandaged arm holding it. My stomach did a looping spiral. *My bloodied arm.*

"You could always hold your arm behind you for the photos," my mother said.

"Or wear long gloves," Nanette suggested.

"For this type of gown?" I said too loudly and flushed. Gloves would look ridiculous. And I'd have to remove the left one to get the ring on.

"The bandage probably looks worse than the scratches," my mom said. "It was just a cat. Take off the bandage."

Carefully, I peeled off the top of the gauze. The scratches flamed deep and red and ugly.

"Oh," my mother said. "Maybe put it back on."

"Too bad it's not a Halloween wedding," Dixie said, and the other two women glared. Dixie shrugged. "What? The weather would be better, and you could wear what you wanted."

I forced a smile and folded the gown over my arm. "It's a minor injury. Accidents happen. It's no big deal. I'm going to try this on."

The gown fit perfectly. My mother and Nanette made all the appropriate noises while Dixie ate a green apple. But their gazes kept traveling to my wounded arm.

But the bandage didn't matter. Arsen would be waiting for me at the altar. That was what counted.

Arsen strolled into the parlor, and Nanette and my mother shrieked. "Get out," Nanette shouted. "You can't see the dress."

Arsen clapped his hands over his eyes and stumbled from the room. "What happened to your arm?" he called from the kitchen. Dixie huffed a laugh.

I slithered from the dress and pulled on my regular clothes. Then I hurried into the kitchen. "It was only a cat." I glanced over my shoulder. None of the other women had followed.

His shoulders relaxed, and he pulled me into his arms. "That's a relief. I thought there might have been more trouble. I didn't want to leave you alone this morning, but your mother insisted."

"There *was* an incident," I admitted. "Someone pulled the fire alarm at the day spa."

He cocked a brow. "At least it wasn't murderous, unless the intent was to get you alone."

I shook my head. "No. That didn't happen. I was with other people the entire time." The fire alarm pull hadn't *felt* like a prank. But how to make him understand, when my own theories were so nebulous?

"But given the timing, it seems a little too coincidental." His arms tightened around me.

My muscles slackened. He understood. I hadn't realized how much I'd feared he wouldn't until this moment.

"What time did this happen?" he asked.

"Eleven-thirty-seven." I'd checked my watch. I lowered my voice. "Arsen, there's something else. Something Nanette—"

The parlor door swung open, and the three women strolled into the kitchen. Dixie warily scanned the kitchen, and her shoulders relaxed.

"The dress is in your closet," my mother said and gave Arsen a severe look. "Where I expect you not to go."

"Yes, ma'am," he said. "Avoid the closet."

"Ugh. I'm going home." Dixie stomped from the kitchen.

"I'm taking Susan for some alone time," Arsen said. "We'll see you two around." Grasping my hand, he led me from the kitchen, but not before I snatched my planners off its small table.

We climbed into Arsen's Jeep Commander. The two of us drove off.

"I hope you don't mind me stealing you away," he said. "But I want to know what happened, in detail. And your mother and Nanette are tough, but they're not me. From now on, we're together, even if I do see your dress and activate a wedding curse."

We drove down thickly wooded residential streets. I ran him through the fire alarm, the cat, and then what Nanette had told me.

His brow wrinkled. "I never knew about a shooting. I'd heard that someone died at their house, but I thought it was an accident."

"It was in the papers."

He made a U-turn. "Then let's hit the *Doyle Times*."

Five minutes later, we pulled up in front of the brick building and walked inside. Tom Tarrant beelined for us through the maze of desks. "Any comment on the latest murder?"

"No," Arsen said shortly. "We're here for the archives."

"Again?" the reporter asked. "So you *do* think these murders are connected to your parents' deaths."

Arsen stiffened. An elderly newspaper man shuffled past.

"I saw what Susan and her friend were looking at," Tom continued.

"And you were eavesdropping," I said sharply.

The reporter grinned. "That too. You got me thinking about Judith and Anabelle and how they quashed that accident investigation. I did more digging after you left, Susan. Not in our archives, in the archives for the paper in Angels Camp. It turns out your parents' accident wasn't the only investigation they suppressed. Did you know Anabelle shot a man in Angels Camp?"

"Yes," Arsen said, terse.

"He broke into their house," Tom continued. "After your parents died, the investigation into what he was doing there went away too."

"Do you have any proof?" Arsen asked.

In response, the reporter pulled a phone from the back pocket of his jeans and tapped on it. "I just sent it to you. I scanned the articles. It's nice to have backups."

My oversized purse pinged, and I extracted my phone. He'd texted several PDF files, which I didn't know how to read on my phone. I forwarded them to my email account. "What are these?" I asked.

"And why do you have Susan in your contacts?" Arsen's gaze hardened.

Tom smiled. "I never delete a contact. You never know when it'll come in handy."

"That's not an answer," Arsen growled.

"Thanks for these." I touched Arsen's arm. "Let's go. We got what we came for." In honesty, I wasn't entirely sure we had. But neither of us wanted to scan through microfiche with Tom Tarrant looking over our shoulders.

Arsen nodded tightly. We walked from the newspaper office.

"I get why you don't like that guy." Arsen helped me into his Jeep Commander, parked beneath a shady elm.

I rolled down the window and drew my computer tablet from my purse, checked my email. The PDF files had come through, and I opened them.

ANGELS CAMP WOMAN SHOOTS, KILLS INTRUDER

ANGELS CAMP, Ca. — A home intruder was shot and killed in Calaveras County Friday night.

Sheriff's deputies reported a woman called 911 just after eleven PM after she heard someone breaking into the house she shared with her sister. After the 42-year-old man, later identified as Perkin Moore, attacked her sister, the woman grabbed a gun and shot him.

More died at the home at 1919 Alameda Drive.

A warm breeze flowed through the open windows. The shadows of the elm leaves shifted across my computer tablet's screen. I opened the second file.

POLICE QUESTION WOMAN'S CLAIM OF SELF DEFENSE

ANGELS CAMP, Ca. — After sheriff's deputies responded to a reported shooting at 1919 Alameda Drive last week, they found the shooter, Anabelle Holiday, claiming to have killed an intruder, Perkin Moore, in defense of her sister, Judith Holiday, who shared the house.

As her story unfolded, police discovered that the intruder was a neighbor, and the sisters had a personal grudge against him due to a property dispute. It is unclear what More was doing in their house.

According to sources, Anabelle claimed she heard the sound of breaking glass downstairs, armed herself, and went to investigate. When Anabelle arrived downstairs, she found More holding a knife and shouting at her sister. When he took a step toward her sister, Anabelle shot him three times.

However, upon arrival at the scene, the police found one set of fresh footprints in the snow leading from the Holiday house to the More house, and two sets of footprints returning. The knife was found at the scene and belonged to Judith Holiday. The investigation is ongoing.

I leaned forward, the seatbelt digging into my chest. The footprints in the snow that Mrs. Steinberg had mentioned. Had Judith brought the man back with her to the house? Had the break-in been faked?

I opened the third article. It was one paragraph, announcing the investigation into the death of Perkin Moore was closed. The article was dated one month after the deaths of Arsen's parents.

I handed the tablet to Arsen, in the driver's seat. He read, his head bowed.

In silence, he returned the tablet to me. "Let's talk to my aunts." He straightened, his mouth set, and started the Jeep.

Chapter 22

"A CAT?"

In the upstairs sitting room, Anabelle shot me a disbelieving look. She leaned forward in her leather armchair. "What were you doing playing with a cat the week before your wedding? *Look* at your poor arm."

Involuntarily, I glanced down at the bandages. The air conditioning—too proper to make so much as a low hum—teased a lock of hair across the back of my neck.

The sitting room was high beamed, and its beamed ceiling was peaked. Like everything else in the house, it was sleek and modern and beautiful and decorated in soft earth tones. A fire crackled in the circular, metal fireplace.

"It doesn't matter." Arsen stood, his back to the picture windows. On the patio beneath, Louis and Nanette lounged in Adirondack chairs. The private golf course and mountains spread out behind them.

"I wasn't playing," I said weakly. "There was a fire. Or not a fire. It turned out someone pulled the fire alarm—"

"It all sounds very silly to me," Anabelle said sternly. "You need to think these things through, especially now that you're becoming a Holiday. And I hope your new gown has sleeves."

"Forget the gown." Judith perched on a cowhide ottoman by the unlit fireplace. "What's this I hear about you two not signing a pre-nuptial agreement?"

I sucked in a breath. A *prenup*? We hadn't even discussed that.

Should I be signing one? I wasn't after Arsen's money and had no plans for getting divorced. But there was an awful lot of money. Maybe I should?

"There's no prenup," Arsen said sharply. "We don't need one."

"You're not thinking with your head," Judith said. "Louis has one ready for you two to sign—"

"Forget it," Arsen said. "You're ducking the questions. Where were you two this morning around eleven, and what happened to Perkin Moore?"

"We were shopping in Doyle," Anabelle said. "We needed to get some last-minute wedding things."

"Together?" Arsen asked.

"That wouldn't have been efficient," Judith said. "Besides, you know how Anabelle dithers."

Her sister tucked in her chin, her graying brows lowering. "I do not."

"And Perkin Moore?" Arsen asked.

"I don't see what that incident—tragic as it was—has to do with anything." Judith straightened on the ottoman. The older woman's mouth pinched, her expression withering.

He folded his arms. "Two people are dead. All these secrets have put Susan in danger."

"Oh! Susan!" Anabelle snorted.

I wilted. Those two words managed to imply that if I'd been a bit smarter, tougher, better, (richer?), there'd have been no problems.

"Money complicates things," Judith told Arsen. "We thought now that you were getting married, you'd finally step up and accept the responsibilities that come with it." She shot me a sidelong glance.

"He's a romantic," Anabelle said bitterly. "It's why he ran off all those years ago. It was always about Susan."

"And look where it's gotten him," her sister said. "A one-man security company. All that wasted potential. You could have done anything."

"He's done quite a lot," I said hotly. "Important things."

But of course, Judith and Anabelle didn't know about his life in the military. He'd always kept it quiet from them for... reasons. Those reasons were making less and less sense to me now.

Judith snorted. "If you'd accepted that scholarship to Harvard and taken your place in the company—"

"How did money complicate things with Perkin Moore?" Arsen asked, his voice hard.

"Ask Susan," Anabelle said, her voice high. "I'm sure she's dug up all sorts of things."

I blinked. *Dug up...?* My face heated. Because I *had* been digging things up. I just hadn't thought they'd resented me for being, well, *me*.

"Were you having an affair with him?" he asked Judith.

She drew back on her seat and sucked in a breath. Judith's angular jaw clamped shut. She glanced at the sitting room's open door.

"So you were," Arsen said. "Was that why he was in your house that night?"

"No," Judith said tightly. "We'd broken it off by then."

"Then why?" he asked. "Why did you go to Perkin's house that night and bring him back with you?"

"I didn't," she said. "Yes, I went to his house to try to get him to help pay for changing the flow of that creek. We argued. I told him I'd sue. We were both... irrationally angry. He'd been drinking. I walked home alone. I don't know what prompted him to break into the house two hours later. More alcohol, I'd presume. Anabelle had no choice in the matter. He would have killed me."

"If it was a simple case of self-defense," Arsen said, "why put pressure on the sheriff to shut down the investigation?"

"Nothing's simple when you have money." Judith rose from the ottoman and rested her hand on the fireplace hood. "Everyone wanted a scandal. Oh, no one *said* it, but that's what they wanted."

"But you didn't have money," Arsen said. "My parents did."

"It didn't matter," Judith said bitterly. "We were Holidays, and Holidays had made it big, and that's all anyone thought about it. It ruined things for us at school. Half our fellow teachers seemed to think we were just playing at our profession." She examined her palm and brushed it off on her slacks.

Anabelle sniffed. "It was very demoralizing. We loved our work."

"Of course we put pressure on the sheriff to drop the case," her sister said. "The entire thing was a witch hunt. So now you see. It can't possibly have anything to do with what's happening now."

"I don't see that at all," Arsen said. "Come on, Susan." He strode toward the open door, and I hurried after him.

"It's not the way I wanted it," Judith said, rising. "We had to protect ourselves. It's the way of the world. Having money changes things. It changes the people who have it, and it changes the people around them who want it. You'll find that out soon enough." She glanced my way.

"It hasn't changed me," Arsen said.

One corner of Judith's mouth lifted. "You think so? You think if you'd grown up like Susan had, you'd be the same person you are today?"

"Let's go," he said gruffly and strode into the high-ceilinged hallway.

I followed him, my insides twisting. *Grown up like Susan had?* "Arsen—"

"They're upset," he said. "And they're frightened. They didn't mean all that stuff about money and you and me."

I darted a glance at Arsen. But they were right, and he knew it. He'd admitted he didn't want the company, the money, to change things. But he knew it would. And had I always been part of that equation?

And... *Harvard?* Could he have gone to Harvard?

He turned to me and rested his hands on my shoulders. "It won't change us. I won't let it."

"But I hadn't considered... If you want me to sign a prenup—"

"No," he exploded. "I told you, I don't care about the money, and I know you don't either. We're not going into our marriage with a divorce contingency plan."

Uncertainly, I nodded. But maybe the money *should* have changed him. Maybe I'd been holding him back all this time.

We walked downstairs and outside to the flagstone patio. Arsen slipped his hand into mine, and I smiled up at him. But I worried.

Nanette twisted in her Adirondack chair. "I was just telling Louis about the excitement at the spa," she said.

"I'm sorry I missed it," he said.

"What were you up to this morning?" I asked lightly.

"Paddleboarding on Lake Alpine," he said. "It was that or hiking, and I didn't feel like hiking alone."

We made more desultory chit-chat, and Arsen and I returned to Wits' End. My parents met us in the B&B's lobby.

"How did it go?" My mother leaned against my old reception desk. "Did anyone break?"

"No," I said.

She cracked her knuckles. "We can take a shot at them if you want."

"No," Arsen said. "Leave them to me."

"It's difficult suspecting family," my father said mildly. He slid a brochure into the rack by the front door. "We love them, even when they're driving us crazy."

Arsen sighed. "I'm not sure who they are anymore."

"Murder will do that," my father said. "But you two will be all right, as long as you stick together."

Arsen slipped his arm around my waist. "Truer words were never spoken." His gaze met mine, and my heart caught. *Together.* Maybe that *was* all we needed.

The moment lengthened, and Arsen smiled. He looked toward my parents. "Is Ghost around?"

"I think he's in the yard." My father nodded toward the kitchen door.

Arsen kissed me. "I'll be right back." He strode into the kitchen. The screen door to the side deck rattled.

My mother's coffee eyes narrowed. "Now. What really happened?"

"Judith and Anabelle were shopping in town, separately," I said. "Louis was paddleboarding up at the lake."

She waved away my explanation. "Oh, that. Well, of course they're still suspects. I'm talking about what happened to *you.* You've been upset, and not by the murder. You *love* murders."

"I don't love murders. They're horrible."

"You know what I mean. What's wrong?"

I clawed a hand through my hair. "Judith said something about money changing things. I don't know. I just assumed Arsen and I would go on as we always had. But he's going to have to get more involved in his parents' company."

When I said it out loud, it didn't sound so bad. So why did I feel so flattened? "I don't know," I finished lamely.

My parents exchanged a look. "People with big money are different," my mother said. "Don't let it bother you."

"Your mother's right," my father said. "The really wealthy aren't like the rest of us. Money changes things. They take the pleasures in life for granted. They assume the worst of human nature, because money tends to bring it out. But that's not you. And it's not Arsen either."

"I know." It wasn't us *now*. But would it be? And how could I be simultaneously worried money would change us, *and* worried Arsen should have embraced the Holiday lifestyle sooner?

My father clapped my shoulder. "Arsen's been dodging the money curse his entire life. I don't expect that to change once you get married."

"Imagine what he would have been like if he'd done what everyone expected." My mother's lip curled. "College first, a cushy corporate job second. How boring."

Walking behind the reception desk, I adjusted an alien bobblehead on its shelf. "They offered him a corporate job after he left the military," I said slowly. "He turned it down." And a Harvard scholarship, apparently.

"That was never Arsen's style," my father said. "And if he'd done it, you two might not be getting married now."

"It all works out for the best," my mother said. "You never would have fit in with that lifestyle."

I straightened a stack of UFO books, nausea churning my gut. But had it worked out for the best? Or had I derailed Arsen's life?

Chapter 23

LOVE'S A FUNNY THING. More than anything, I wanted to be married to Arsen. And more than anything, I wanted what was best for him, what would make him happy. If those two desires conflicted... I swallowed.

I wanted to think Arsen knew his own mind. And he did. He wouldn't have asked to marry me if he hadn't meant it. But he was also loyal. Had his loyalty to me clouded his judgment?

My cell phone rang on the small kitchen table. Eyes hot, I checked the number. "It's Sarah."

"Your neighbor?" My mother pulled out a chair and sat across from me, her back to the stove. "I don't think you have time for her now." Beneath the table, the beagle sneezed.

Maybe not, but it made an excellent distraction. "Hi, Sarah," I answered. "What's up?"

"I'm sorry to bother you, but my rooster seems to have left the yard. I don't suppose you've seen him around?"

The back of my neck tightened. I studied my parents.

My father leaned against the butcher block counter and investigated the inside of his empty mug. My mother's expression was bland.

"No," I said. "I haven't. But I'll go outside and check now."

"Oh, thank you. I'd like to think he's smart enough to return on his own. But I think that would be giving Fred too much credit." She laughed.

"Right. I'll check and get back to you." I hung up. My mouth pinched. "Sarah's rooster's gone missing."

"How dreadful," my mother said dryly.

"I'm sure he'll turn up," my father said, still frowning into his mug. "Is there any coffee?"

"Where is he?" I asked.

My mother's eyes widened. "How should I know?"

"You've been threatening to do something about that rooster since you got here." I crossed my arms.

"And we promised we'd stop," my mother said.

My eyes narrowed. "Did you?" My parents could be tricky about how they worded their promises.

"A coyote probably got him." My father wandered to the empty coffeepot. "I heard some howling behind the B&B last night."

I rose from the table and pocketed my phone. "I'm going to see if Fred's wandered into the yard."

"I suppose if he *had* wandered into your yard," my mother said, "he would be fair game."

"No," I said. "No, he wouldn't be." I stormed from the kitchen and onto the side porch. Bailey trotted after me.

Arsen and Ghost stood beside the gazebo covered in climbing roses. Ghost hung his head. Arsen clapped him on the shoulder.

I walked down the porch steps. Bailey whined behind me.

"Honestly," I told the beagle. "It's only three steps." But I returned to the porch, picked him up, and carried him to the lawn. I set the dog down. "Catch the scent of any roosters?"

He huffed and shook himself, his collar jingling. The graying beagle trotted to the spirit house beside my other neighbor's picket fence.

The two men walked toward me. "Everything okay?" Arsen asked. A breeze stirred the pines, and they whispered a response.

"Aside from the murders?" I asked shakily.

His smile was rueful. "Aside from that."

"Sarah's missing her rooster," I said. "She thought it might have gotten into my yard."

"I haven't seen one," Ghost said. "Have you, er, heard from your cousin?"

"As of this morning you were still officially a jerk," I said. "And I don't blame her for thinking that. You catfished Dixie."

He winced. "A lot of my friends call me Steve. I wasn't trying to pull anything over on her."

"And bailing on Vegas?"

Ghost flushed. "A buddy of mine got in trouble. I had to go help him out."

Oh, brother. No wonder Dixie hadn't accepted *that* excuse. "And not calling her afterward?"

"Okay that was... It's not what it looks like."

"That explains everything." I folded my arms.

"We served together," he said. "It's about loyalty."

My throat tightened. "Yeah. But Dixie deserves loyalty too. I get that you two were at the beginning of things, but ditching her like that wasn't a good start. Pretending you were someone else when you got here didn't exactly build trust."

He rubbed the back of his neck. "I didn't think she'd want to have anything to do with me if she knew I was that Steve."

"You were probably right on that count, buddy," Arsen said.

"I'm going to look for that rooster." I walked down the lawn toward the gazebo. A small brown bird splashed in the UFO fountain.

Arsen jogged to my side. "Hey. You okay?"

"No. I'm sorry, I know I should say everything's great, I'll be fine, we're getting married in three days. But two of our guests are dead. I look like an escapee from a slasher film with this arm. Your mother's beautiful dress was ruined by someone who may or may not be a killer. And I don't fit into your family. When it was just you and me and your aunts, I told myself they were lovely, and everything was fine. And heaven knows my family has its own challenges. I mean my *parents*. Ha. They've probably buried that rooster where no one will ever find it. And you've got this whole alternate life you could have had. But you're with me instead, and I'm starting to wonder why."

"Because I love you. I can't imagine life without you."

I rubbed my brow. "Really? You can't imagine life as a high-powered executive with in-laws that don't try to assassinate harmless roosters? Or a wife who plans everything within an inch of its life? Not that my planning has done much good lately," I muttered.

His brow wrinkled. "Are you having second thoughts?"

"No." Briefly, I closed my eyes. "My only thought is I want you to be happy."

"Being with you makes me happy. You ground me, Susan. And you do it in a way that's never boring. Are we okay?"

I nodded. He kissed me until the porch screen door banged, and my parents emerged from the Victorian.

Arsen smiled. "Let's find that rooster."

We did not find the rooster. I did, however, call the man who rented paddleboards out at Lake Alpine. He confirmed Louis had rented a board at ten AM and returned it just before noon today. So that was that.

And then we returned to the mansion for a gloomy family dinner al fresco by the aunts' pool. Dixie didn't show up. Ghost picked at his steak. Anabelle kept sighing about my arm, though Judith did apologize for being so hard on me earlier. And my parents wouldn't stop making comments about rich people they'd known who'd come to bad ends.

I suspected they might have helped more than a few of those rich people along.

After dinner, Arsen and I drifted away from the others. We stood at the low stone wall and gazed at the stars. A dark, flat circle marked the new moon in the sky.

"The lights from the house are dulling them." Behind me, he slipped his arms around my waist. "We'd see more away in the mountains."

I sighed. There was a metaphor in their somewhere. But I didn't explore it. I rested against his strong form.

"Oh, Arsen," Anabelle trilled. "Would you help me with a box?"

Arsen kissed my temple. "I'll be right back." He strode away.

I stared at the carpet of stars. Even dimmed by the house lights, they were brighter than anything you'd see in a city.

"It's a lot to take, isn't it?" Louis asked from beside me, and I started.

I laughed slightly. "I didn't hear you walk up."

"It's my catlike stealth," he joked. "How are you holding up?"

"Better than Sophie and Junior." My hands dropped to my sides. It would be churlish to complain about my little problems in the face of those lives taken.

"Good," he said. "You're tough. But that comes as no surprise."

"Thanks. I think."

The lawyer slipped his hands into the pockets of his charcoal trousers. He tilted his silvering head toward the sky. "None of us started out with money, you know. All we had was drive and determination."

I smiled. "Are you trying to tell me something?"

"Don't let us intimidate you," he said. "Sometimes we forget what it was like, being young and just finding our footing." He nodded toward my bandaged arm. "You belong here, cat scratches or no."

I rubbed my bandage. The scratches were starting to itch.

"Judith told me you two are hesitating on the prenuptial agreement," he said. "I know they're not very romantic. But they can help open up clear communication channels regarding financial expectations."

"I'm not sure why Judith's involved in this," I said, and immediately regretted my harsh tone.

The lawyer raised his hands in a warding gesture. "She's not. This is between you and Arsen, of course."

Arsen returned to my side. "What's between Susan and me?"

"We were just discussing the prenuptial agreement," Louis said.

Arsen's expression darkened. "We don't need one."

"Your parents had one," Louis said.

Arsen blinked. "What?"

"Your mother insisted on it," he said. "It was her money that initially financed the company. Not that there was very much of it, and not that your mother cared about that. She just wanted to keep things clean and clear."

"I didn't know that." Arsen's tanned brow wrinkled.

Louis motioned toward the mansion, glowing with light. "I suppose you could say all this was really hers, or due to her. She was the majority shareholder in the company and kept a tight eye on the finances. Not that any of that matters. It's yours now. Anyway, the prenup is up to you two." He moved toward Nanette, standing at the other end of the lit pool.

"I guess that explains why they thought I'd take the house after we married." Furrows appeared between Arsen's brows. "It wasn't my father's. His sisters have no claim to the house."

"Of course it was your father's," I said. "Your parents were married. It belonged to them both. They built the company together. So what if one put in sweat equity and the other put in cash?"

"My aunts wouldn't see it that way."

I bit the inside of my lip. And how had they seen it all those years ago? Moving into a home that they thought belonged to their dead sister-in-law? And how had Arsen's mother felt about spending company resources to smooth over the death of Perkin Moore?

"Susan." He swallowed and didn't meet my eyes. "Something *has* changed."

I stilled.

"I'm starting to wonder," he said, "if one of my aunts is a killer."

Chapter 24

Arsen's expression turned anguished. Reflected, watery light from the swimming pool wavered across his handsome face. His aunts, the women who'd raised him, were suspects, and he knew it. And they were the only parents he'd really known.

And suddenly, none of this was about me. All my insecurities, the dress, the arm, the prenup, none of it mattered. I'd known that this was hitting Arsen hard, but that had been one worry amidst many. Now it was the only thing that mattered.

I took his hand. "Maybe they are suspects," I said. "I hope not. But whatever comes, we'll get through this."

"I know." He enfolded me in his arms. Crickets chirped. We stood there, our faces turned away from the mansion. Stars brightened overhead. The Sierra night cooled.

And then we returned to Wits' End. And after my parents with exaggerated yawns went to bed, and Ghost vanished into his own room, Arsen stayed with me.

The next morning, the two of us lounged in the Wits' End gazebo drinking coffee. The scent of roses twined about us. I relaxed on the bench, Arsen's arm over my shoulder.

Dixie stomped across the Victorian's lawn. Ignoring us, she climbed the porch steps and vanished into the kitchen. A low woof emerged from the B&B, a greeting from Bailey.

"Think she's here for breakfast?" Arsen asked.

"I think that's her excuse. She's probably telling herself Ghost's not going to knock her off her routine." My pulse slowed. Dixie'd been acting like his betrayal was no big thing. But I could tell this business with Ghost had stung. Badly.

Arsen sipped his coffee. "What's on the agenda for today?"

Chase RSVP stragglers. Get the ring cleaned. Practice our vows. It was all in the planner. And none of it mattered. "Nothing," I said.

He raised a brow. "Nothing?"

"Well, there's one thing. We need to find out where everyone was the evening your parents were killed."

Arsen set his mug on the white-painted railing, his rugged face set and serious. His ankle rested over his knee, creasing his khaki slacks.

I held my breath. He'd told me he was all in on the investigation, but he loved his aunts. And our investigation had unearthed unsettling truths about his family.

A bird chirped in a nearby pine. The UFO fountain splashed.

He nodded. "Makes sense. But that was over twenty years ago. What are the odds they'll remember where they were?"

I exhaled slowly. "They'll know. Everyone remembers where they were when tragedies struck. Ask anyone alive at the time where they were on September 11th. They'll tell you exactly where they were and what they were doing."

"And it can't hurt to try."

"What will our excuse be for asking?"

"At this point," he said, "I don't think we need one. I can just tell them I want to know more about that day. They can't exactly turn me down. And we do this together. I'm not letting you out of my sight until the wedding."

"Good. I want to be with you."

"What do we tell the others though?" He nodded toward the two-story Victorian.

"Do we have to tell them anything?"

He grinned. "Let's go."

Leaving the rest to their own devices, Arsen and I fled in his Jeep up the mountain to the mansion. It was still early, and Arsen let himself in with his key.

The modern mansion's high ceilings and wide marble hallways were empty and silent. Arsen and I tiptoed to the back patio so as not to wake anyone. We waited in two Adirondack chairs for the others to emerge from their rooms.

The sun rose higher over the eastern mountains. Arsen pushed his sunglasses onto the top of his whiskey-colored hair and squinted. "I used to love it here."

"You don't anymore?"

"It doesn't feel like home anymore." He smiled at me. "Wits' End does."

"Will you feel the same with guests trooping in and out?"

"I don't mind company," he said, "as long as I have a place alone with you." His hazel eyes grew serious.

Water lapped at the edges of the rectangular pool. And suddenly I wanted to join him in his chair and peel his golf shirt off his muscular chest. But knowing my luck, that would be exactly the moment someone exited the house. So I leaned back in my chair instead and studied the cloudless sky.

A glass door slid open behind us. "Arsen? Susan?" Louis, in neat navy slacks and a white button-up shirt, joined us by the pool. He scraped an Adirondack chair across the paving stones and sat. "You're here early. Or did I forget about an excursion?" He wore his sunglasses on the top of his head, like Arsen.

"Not this early," I said. "We're having a relaxing morning."

Louis flashed a smile. "I like the way your mind works. I was thinking of getting back on Lake Alpine for more paddleboarding. It's peaceful out there."

"Did my parents go to the lake often?" Arsen asked.

"Oh, yes. Not for paddleboarding, of course. That wasn't a thing back then. But to swim and boat. I had many perfect afternoons with them on the lake." He shook his silver-haired head. "This visit has brought back all sorts of memories."

"I've been thinking a lot about them too," Arsen said. "Especially about how they died."

"Don't think about it," Louis said. "We try to rationalize accidents away, but sometimes they just happen."

"It must have been a blow for you too." I crossed my ankles. "You were so close."

"It was." The lawyer rose from his chair. He walked to the pool and stared across its blue water. "They were my best friends."

"We were reading one of the old newspaper articles about their deaths," I said. "It mentioned someone from the company had been at the house the day of the accident. Was that you?"

"Yes," he said sadly. "I had some papers for them to deal with. We'd just begun expanding production. There was a lease for a new property they needed to sign."

"They?" Arsen asked.

The lawyer laughed shortly. "Bergdis wasn't exactly a silent part-ner."

Good for her. I shifted in the wooden chair.

"And that day they seemed normal to you?" Arsen asked.

Louis turned to face us and folded his arms. "Well, no. There was some strain between them and Judith. A separate legal matter she was involved in."

"The death of Perkin Moore," I said.

Louis's blue-gray eyes widened slightly. "You know about that?"

Arsen nodded. "My aunts told us."

"Ah." The lawyer grimaced and sat on the low stone wall beside our chairs. "Well, I was the fool who'd suggested getting a PI. I'm not a criminal attorney, and I told John that and to hire a specialist. He decided to hold off on getting another attorney until and unless Judith was actually charged. But I knew a PI, and so John hired him. Judith was furious. Bergdis was furious too."

"Why was my mother angry about the PI?"

Louis rested his elbows on his thighs. His hands dangled loosely. "She kept a tight hand on company resources, and rightly so. The company had been making waves in the industry. We were a private firm on the verge of an even bigger breakthrough, and finances were... complicated."

"And Judith?" I asked.

"She seemed to think the whole thing would blow over, and we were wasting money." Louis slipped his sunglasses down over his eyes. "The man had been in their house, after all. It was a clear case of self-defense."

"Was it?" Arsen asked. "The newspaper articles made it seem like there might have been more to it."

"Reporters." One corner of his mouth crooked. "If it bleeds, it leads. They're always looking for a sensational angle, aren't they? Especially when someone with money's involved."

The sun rose higher above the mountains. Squinting, I raised my hand to block the light. "When did you last see Arsen's parents?" I asked him.

"That afternoon. It was around four, I think, when I finally left. The sheriff asked me about it, about them, how they'd seemed. They hadn't been drinking. I suppose they could have started after I left. But the autopsies proved there was no alcohol in their systems. It was just a terrible, terrible tragedy."

"And they left the house at five-forty," I murmured. Well after Louis had departed. But did it matter? What was I thinking? That someone had run them off the road? Rigged their brakes to fail?

"What?" Louis asked.

"You must have been nearly to Sacramento by the time of the crash," I said.

"Yes," he said absently. "I suppose so. I didn't hear about it until later, of course."

"How much later?" Arsen asked.

"The next day. Nanette called me."

"Where was Nanette when this happened?" I asked.

"Didn't you know?" Louis said. "She was here, at the mansion."

Chapter 25

THE MANSION'S TALL WINDOWS turned to sheets of copper fire. Sunlight glinted off the swimming pool and made twisting golden darts of the rippling reflections.

"What was Nanette doing here that day?" I asked.

On the low, stone wall, Louis shrugged. The motion barely made a ripple in the white fabric of his shirt. "Something to do with the sisters as well. You have to understand, family meant everything to John. If it was between the company and saving his sisters from being railroaded, there was no contest."

"And Nanette didn't approve," Arsen said slowly.

"We'd all put our hearts into the company," Louis said. "Of course we didn't want to see Judith and Anabelle go down for a murder they hadn't committed. But we didn't want to lose everything we'd worked so hard for either."

"Nanette and my mother were in agreement then," Arsen said.

Louis chuckled. "They were quite a force individually. Together, you can imagine."

"Yes, I can." Casually, Arsen rested his hand on the arm of my chair.

I grasped his broad hand. "And after John and Bergdis died?" I asked. "The company went on in spite of everything. Judith and

Anabelle weren't prosecuted. It sounds like everyone was worried about nothing." Not that I was judging. I worried about nothing on a regular basis.

"Not nothing," Louis said. "The company went on through sheer luck and grit. Judith and Anabelle had been granted charge over the shares Arsen had inherited. They insisted on setting a sizable amount aside for his care immediately. It made things difficult. But Nanette got us through."

Arsen frowned. "For my care?"

"Payments to keep up the house, that sort of thing," Louis said. "They didn't want to lose the home your parents had built here. And now, in hindsight, I can't say as I blame them. Of course at the time it seemed mad."

I studied the paving stones. I'd always liked Arsen's aunts. But I realized now that I'd liked them more in theory—as fun older relatives. I'd never really known them as human beings with fears and desires and heartaches.

I ran my hand up Arsen's forearm. His muscles were hard and tight.

"So what's on the agenda for today?" Louis asked.

"Wine tasting," I said absently.

He arched a brow. "Anything good grown up here?"

"Plenty," Arsen said. "But you'll decide for yourself."

We trailed after him into the spacious breakfast room. Heads together, Judith and Anabelle sat at a long, rectangular table beside an unlit fireplace. They jerked apart when they noticed us.

"You're here early," Judith said warily.

Louis wandered to the buffet on the long bar. Arsen pulled out a chair for me at their table, and I sat. The table was gorgeous, a river of sparkling blue resin running down its middle. I ran my hand along its smooth, epoxied surface.

"Tell us about the argument you had with my parents the day they died," Arsen said.

Anabelle blanched. Her long gray hair was done up in loose coils at the top of her head. "Arsen, you can't possibly think—"

"I don't think anything," he said quietly. "I don't know anything. I get why you kept this from me when I was a kid. I wouldn't have understood it anyway. But two more people are dead, and it's connected. It's all connected. I can feel it. What happened that day?" He sat beside me. Beneath the table, I laced my fingers between his.

"You can't know they're connected," Anabelle said. "They can't be. How can they?"

Silverware clattered at the buffet. I glanced at Louis, piling fruit on his plate.

"Because Sophie had no real connection to Doyle outside of this family," I said. "And she was here, in this house, the day Arsen's parents died. She may have known something, seen something..."

The two women shared a look. "Sophie was a lovely girl," Anabelle said weakly.

"The argument," Arsen said. "What happened?"

Judith exhaled loudly. "John thought he was doing me a favor. He wasn't. I didn't want a PI digging into my life. Was that so much to ask?"

"Why?" I asked. "What did you think he'd find?"

"My private life is nobody's business but my own. It was a waste of time and money." Judith's angular jaw thrust forward, mulish. "Bergdis wasn't happy about hiring a PI either."

"Why not?" I asked.

"Because they were using company funds," Judith said.

"Louis didn't seem to have a problem with it," Arsen said.

"He changed his tune once Bergdis put her foot down," Judith said in a low voice. She glanced toward the bar. Louis filled a champagne flute with orange juice. "But he'd always go along with anything she suggested."

Arsen's hazel eyes narrowed. "What are *you* suggesting?"

"Nothing," Anabelle said quickly. "There was nothing between Bergdis and Louis. She only had eyes for your father. Louis was just her faithful knight. Always chivalrous. She even called him that, her *faithful knight*."

That tracked with what Nanette had said at the spa. *Poor Louis.* Was there anything worse than unrequited love? But had Nanette been its victim as well? Louis had seemed to hint she'd been in love with Arsen's father.

Louis walked to our table. "Ladies, can I get you anything? Another mimosa?"

Anabelle blushed. "No, thank you."

"Sophie was seen talking to Junior," I said. "Did any of you see them later, or happen to overhear their conversation?"

"Not me." Louis pulled out a chair and sat. "Why?"

"Junior seemed pretty full of himself before he died," I said. "Like he knew something. I wonder if Sophie told him something before she died."

"And that's why he was killed?" Anabelle asked. "But what could Sophie possibly know?"

"She was here the night Arsen's parents died," I said. "You said she was feeling guilty about the accident. Are you sure she felt guilty about not stopping them from leaving? Or could it have been about something else?"

Anabelle cocked her head, her loose pile of hair listing slightly. "I don't... Actually, I don't know exactly why she felt guilty. I just assumed... She wasn't responsible for that accident. She couldn't have been. It seemed like misplaced guilt to me."

"Maybe it wasn't so misplaced," Arsen said.

"What are you suggesting?" Judith asked. "That Sophie somehow drove them off the road?"

Arsen shook his head. "The police report on the accident didn't mention evidence of any other cars involved."

I shot him a sharp look. Could we trust the police report? Because it didn't sound like the old sheriff had been terribly honest or competent.

Anabelle pressed a plump hand to her mouth. "You read the accident report?" she breathed. "Oh, Arsen. I'm so sorry."

"Judith?" I asked. "What do you remember Sophie saying the evening she arrived for our wedding? Exactly."

Twin furrows appeared between her gray brows. "She said she felt terrible about what happened. She said... she should have known something was wrong."

"Did she say why?" Arsen asked.

"No," Judith said. "And I didn't press. It seemed ridiculous, like she was dredging up the past to recreate a sense of drama. I found it distasteful, unhelpful."

Louis relaxed in his high-backed chair. "Still... Could Sophie have seen something that day? Something that indicated there was more to that car accident than bad luck?"

Judith shook her head. "We'll probably never know."

"Oh, yes we will," I said. We were going to figure this out because we had to. Arsen deserved to know the truth. He squeezed my hand lightly.

Louis smiled. "I like your confidence. You're so like Bergdis."

"You had a bit of a crush on her," Anabelle said to Louis and laid her wrinkled hand atop his. "It's all right. Everyone loved her."

He looked down at his plate, piled high with fruit and eggs and sausages. "I suppose I did. She was very..." He cleared his throat. "A remarkable woman, your mother."

Nanette breezed into the room. "No more of your Bergdis obsession. The happy couple doesn't need to hear our sad stories." She rested her hand on Arsen's shoulder. "For a moment..." She cleared her throat. "For a moment, from the back, when I walked in here I thought I was looking at John and Bergdis."

"There is a similarity," Anabelle said. "Arsen looks so like John. And Susan with that head of blond hair..."

"It's lovely to see you two together," Nanette said. "But it's a little early for wine tasting. Where are the others?"

"Back at Wits' End," Arsen said. "We'll meet them at the winery later. We had time to kill and wanted to swing by."

"Susan?" Nanette said. "Are you all right? You look... intense. Or maybe intent."

I started. "What? Oh. I'm fine, thanks."

Looking at us from the back... The thought fled, leaving me stumped. Nanette had triggered an idea... a... something. I grimaced and gave a small headshake. Had I been looking at things all wrong?

Chapter 26

I STARED AT MY kitchen. Every available surface was covered in tiny jade plants in terracotta pots. I blinked away tears. My friend Jayce had done it. She'd pulled off new wedding favors. And the rustic look of the pots was perfect.

My mother leaned against the butcher block counter. "Personally, I find giving guests plants a bit odd. Caring for a plant is a lot of responsibility. Not everyone wants it."

"No," I said, "it's perfect. Jade plants are hard to kill. They don't need a lot of water, just sunlight."

My mother folded her arms. "I don't want a plant."

"What about a rooster?" I asked sharply. My neighbor's rooster *still* hadn't turned up.

She sniffed. "I told you, I had nothing to do with that bird going missing. There are all sorts of predators in the mountains. It's a wonder more of her chickens haven't been taken. But since we're talking about murder—"

"So you *did* murder that rooster."

"No," she said. "I'm presuming another animal committed the crime. I'm talking about your murders."

"They're not mine."

She walked to the empty coffee pot by the sink, picked it up, put it down again. "They're certainly putting a damper on the wedding."

"Also," I said acidly, "two innocent lives were taken."

"We don't know how innocent they were, but I take your point. Now, who did it?"

"How should I know?"

Her eyes narrowed. "You know *something*, young lady. I could always tell when you were hiding things from me."

I *really* hoped that wasn't true. "All right. Here are our suspects." I plucked a short, round-shaped jade plant off the counter. "Anabelle. I hate to suspect one of Arsen's aunts. But several months before Arsen's parents were killed, she shot a man. He'd supposedly broken into their house."

"Really?" my mother said, looking impressed. "It's always the ones who look innocent you have to watch."

"She wasn't charged. It was ruled self-defense. But there's something sketchy about it all. I hate to say it, but Anabelle had means, motive and opportunity for these two murders." If one of Arsen's aunts was a killer... What if *both* were?

"What motive?" my mother asked.

I shook myself. "There may have been some sort of cover-up about that man she shot. Arsen's father hired a PI to investigate, to try to get them off. But Judith shut the whole thing down. She didn't want an investigation."

"She was hiding something."

"It could have been something that looked incriminating but really wasn't," I said. "Apparently Judith did have a romantic relationship with the man at one point."

And then there was that business with the footprints in the snow. Could Judith have brought the man back to her house to make it *look* like a break-in?

"And then after Arsen's parents died," I continued, "their problems went away. They moved into the mansion and got control over a lot of money."

"So she had multiple motives. And of course, Judith has just as much motive as Anabelle."

I plucked a taller, skinnier jade plant from the counter. "Exactly." Edging plants together on the table to make space, I set my Anabelle and Judith plants down. "And then I learned both Nanette and Louis were in Doyle when Arsen's parents were killed." I found two elegant-looking jade plants and picked them up.

My mother shook her head. "You were with Nanette when that fire alarm was pulled. And what are you doing with those plants?"

"I'm using them as visual representations of our suspects."

"Why?"

"Because," I sputtered. "They're visual representations." It seemed obvious to me.

"There are only three suspects. I think we can keep them in our heads without resorting to houseplants. Nanette couldn't have pulled that fire alarm at the spa. You were with her."

"The fire alarm could have been a fluke," I said weakly. "A coincidence."

She raised her brows. "There are no coincidences in our world, my dear. Only seeming coincidences which are really threats in disguise."

"That's not my world." And what about good coincidences? What about serendipity and magic, and... And when had I started believing in magic? Now I was just being contrary.

My mother opened a blue-painted cupboard and extracted a bag of coffee beans. "Says the woman up to her neck in corpses. And it's less than forty-eight hours until your wedding. Who knows how many more people will die?" she said with relish. "I suppose you thought Nanette's motive for killing the Holidays was getting control of the company?"

"Yes."

"And Louis?" She found the coffee grinder and poured beans into the top.

"That one's—"

Whirrrrr. I winced.

"...shakier," I finished when the grinding stopped. "But it seems they were worried that John's spending to clear his sisters' names impacted the company finances."

"And Louis couldn't find another job?" She dumped the ground beans into a filter. "No. That's too weak. Besides, Louis was in love with Bergdis."

"You knew about that?" I asked, surprised.

"I haven't been letting the grass grow under my feet. I know how to conduct a *discreet* interrogation."

I sucked in my cheeks. My interrogations were plenty discreet. "That's—"

Arsen strolled into the kitchen. "Good, you're here."

"And that's my cue to leave," she said.

I motioned toward the counter. "What about your—?"

My mother strode out the porch door.

Coffee?

Arsen frowned. "Did I do something wrong?"

I sighed and leaned against his muscular frame. "No. She's trying to be *discreet.*"

He laughed softly and wrapped his arms around me. "We're getting married in two days. Why bother?"

"You know my mother."

"Not really," he said. "Your parents made it clear they didn't want me in their business. And I don't ask questions."

"I'm sorry," I mumbled into his broad chest. Why did my parents have to be so... dangerous? Irritating? Nuts?

"Don't be. I thought I knew my aunts. Now I realize I didn't know them at all. I always saw them as friendly parental figures. I guess I never really saw them as people until now."

"It's strange. I was just thinking the same thing. Not the parental-figure part, but that I just saw them as two aunts, not as two full people."

"I'm sorry about all this," he said. "I wanted you to have the perfect wedding."

I'd wanted that too, along with my happily ever after. But those things weren't real, because nothing in life was perfect. There was beauty and wonder and love, and measures of darkness and violence and pain. And all we could do was accept that which we couldn't control. Like how the people in his wealthy circles perceived me.

All I wanted now, all I could do, was to have Arsen's back. I would do everything I could to help get him through whatever came our way. "I don't care about the wedding. It's the marriage that counts."

And then he kissed me.

At the end of the long, wooden bar, Dixie, in shorts and a black tank, gulped down her tasting. The brown-haired hostess shot her a startled look. "This is a Zinfandel with a bouquet of—"

"Don't care." Dixie tapped the rim of her empty goblet. "Hit me."

At the opposite end of the bar, Ghost stared glumly into his untouched glass.

From my spot beside a cheese and cracker table, I sighed. Those two *still* weren't speaking? "I feel like I should fix this," I told Arsen and rubbed my thumb along the rim of my goblet. "But I don't know how."

He laid a hand on my shoulder. "Nah. They need to figure it out for themselves. Or not." He sipped his wine.

I nodded. I hated watching people make mistakes. But maybe it wasn't a mistake. Maybe Dixie was right to steer clear of Ghost.

There was a roar of laughter from the bar. Judith slapped Nanette's back, and the two women toasted each other. Louis shook his head. Chuckling, Anabelle made her way to us beside black shelves filled with cheese knives and mustard jars.

"This was exactly what everyone needed," Anabelle said. "I haven't been to a wine tasting in years."

"It seemed a shame not to take advantage of the local wineries." I sipped my Cabernet.

"As long as everyone gets home safely," Anabelle said. "We don't want a—" She paled and bit her plump lip.

"Another accident?" Arsen asked. "Don't worry. I'll make sure there are no drunk drivers on the road today."

"I shouldn't have brought it up." Anabelle plucked a bag of dip mix from a black cardboard display and studied it. "But lately I haven't been able to stop thinking about that day."

"Have you remembered anything more?" Arsen asked.

"No." She returned the mix to the display stand. "But I always remember it perfectly. It was too awful to forget."

"Did you know about Arsen's mother accusing Sophie of theft?" I asked her.

She grimaced. "Oh. That. Bergdis was horribly embarrassed about it."

"Is that why Sophie stayed on after the accusation?" I asked. "Bergdis apologized?"

"She must have," Anabelle said. "I would have a hard time staying in a place where I'd been accused of theft. And like I said, Bergdis was so embarrassed. She confessed to me the next day she'd made a scene."

"What was stolen?" Arsen asked.

Anabelle tapped her rounded chin. "You know, I don't think she told me what was taken."

"Lingerie." I shot an apologetic smile at Arsen. I hadn't meant to keep it a secret. But there'd been so much going on, that detail had slipped my mind. And we hadn't had a chance to really go through the notes in my planner.

Anabelle blinked. "Oh. That explains why she thought Sophie had taken it. She was the only other woman staying in the house. Bergdis must have misplaced it and found it later. But Louis smoothed everything over."

"Louis did?" I asked.

"He was always Bergdis's fixer. I suspect there may have been some money involved."

"You mean he paid Sophie not to leave in a huff?" Arsen asked.

At the counter, the hostess boxed a case of wine for my mother. Ghost rose from his seat.

I nudged Arsen. "It looks like we're wrapping up here." I moved toward Dixie.

Ghost beat me to her. "Can I drive you to the next winery?" he asked.

"No." Dixie didn't meet his gaze.

"It's just that maybe you shouldn't be driving," he said in a low voice.

"And I won't be." She slid off her barstool. "I'm walking home."

"You're not coming to the next winery?" I asked, disappointed. If my cousin was this miserable around Ghost, it wouldn't be fair to torture her. I'd just hoped she'd be a little *less* miserable.

"Nah," she said. "I've got things to do."

"Have you practiced the wedding prayer?" I asked.

She stared blankly. "Wedding prayer?"

"You know," I said. "The prayer at the reception. Don't tell me you don't have it ready?"

"I guess rub-a-dub-dub, thanks for the grub won't cut it," she said.

"No," I said frostily.

"I can help," Ghost said. "I'm pretty good at speeches."

My cousin stared coldly. "Yeah. You are." She walked out the tasting room's front door.

Chapter 27

"I, SUSAN, TAKE THEE, Arsen, to be my wedded husband." My voice trembled. "To have and to hold, from this day forward, for better, for worse, for richer, for poorer, in sickness and in health, to love and to cherish, till death do us part."

Arsen smiled down at me, his gaze soft. One side of his collar was tucked oddly inside his golf shirt, and I longed to fix it. Not because I cared about the shirt—this was only a rehearsal. But because I wanted to feel his skin beneath my fingers.

A warm afternoon breeze stirred the pines on the nearby hillside. The gazebo's climbing roses fluttered. Their scent in the gazebo grew heady.

The pastor, in a t-shirt and jeans, cleared his throat. "Then you'll exchange rings. Did you want to practice that?"

"Uh, I didn't bring them," Arsen said.

The pastor nodded. "Okay then, you may kiss the bride."

Arsen pulled me close and softly kissed my lips. And even though he'd kissed me many times before, even though this was only a day-before-the-wedding run-through, my heart thundered in my ears. We broke apart, my knees wobbly. Arsen swallowed.

On the lawn, my parents applauded. His aunts sniffed. Our two witnesses, Louis and Nanette grinned.

"And then I'll pronounce you husband and wife and say a few words," the pastor said, brisk. "After that, you'll exit the gazebo in the reverse order you entered it. Susan and Arsen, you two go first. Then Dixie and Gho— uh, Estevan."

Dixie's brows drew downward. She folded her arms.

But I didn't care. I was too happy in that moment to worry about Dixie's love life. My heart was full of the belief that everything would work out for the best. And tomorrow, Arsen and I would be married. *Tomorrow.*

He took my hand. We walked down the gazebo steps and stopped beside the UFO fountain.

Ghost moved toward Dixie. She glared, and he took a hasty step back. Stiffly, the two followed us.

"Are we done?" Dixie said.

The pastor closed his Bible. "I am. I'm sorry, I have to run. I've got to meet another parishioner shortly. I'll see you two tomorrow at eleven."

"Thank you," Arsen told him.

"Weddings are my favorite part of the job." He smiled and strode down the lawn.

Dixie headed into the Victorian.

"She isn't going to forgive me, is she?" Ghost asked.

"The bigger the crime, the bigger the grovel required," I said. "It has to be proportional."

"She's right, man." Arsen clapped his friend's shoulder. "It's a rule."

Ghost scowled. "Who made a rule like that?"

"It's a universal," I said. "And it's only logical. And fair. But if you don't think Dixie's worth it, then don't bother. She deserves something real. Some*one* real."

Ghost gloomily raked a hand through his near-black hair. "Yeah. She does."

My parents ambled to the base of the gazebo. My father's stomach rumbled loudly. "Rehearsal dinner?"

"Susan and I will meet you at Alchemy," Arsen said. "We've got some last-minute things to do."

I frowned. We did? I was sure our schedule was clear. Had the wedding pressure finally gotten to me? Was I off schedule? "My planners are inside. I'll be right back."

"I'll come with you." Arsen grasped my hand and stopped me. "Ghost, get everyone to Alchemy, would you? Take my car." He tossed his keys to his friend. Ghost caught them one-handed.

We hurried toward the house. "What did I forget?" I asked. "I thought we'd scheduled going directly to Alchemy."

"Alchemy can wait. I need to be alone with you." His look smoldered. "And not to talk."

We lay tangled on the black velvet couch in my parlor. Arsen's chest rose and fell. "Are you ready to be married?" he asked.

"I can't wait to be married to you." So it was a good thing it was happening tomorrow. *Tomorrow.* I shivered.

He pulled the white throw blanket over my shoulders. "Are you okay?"

I tugged the soft blanket tighter. "Of course. You?"

Arsen hesitated. "I just have this feeling..." He shook his head.

"That something else is going to happen."

His arms tightened around me. "Yes."

I twisted the glittering ring on my finger. "Are we doing the right thing? Not about getting married. Someone could set the gazebo on fire for all I care. We're still getting married. But the wedding, bringing everyone here. Is it a mistake?"

He shifted on the velvet couch. "Whatever's going on, it's not some maniac obsessed with killing wedding guests."

I thought so too. But what if we were wrong? "How did your background search go?"

He sighed. "Nanette likes to gamble."

Whoa. I hadn't guessed anything like that. "Too much?"

"It's hard to tell. And there was a sexual harassment complaint lodged against Louis a few years ago. But it was dropped."

"Who made the complaint?" I asked.

"The company kept the woman's name confidential. I couldn't get at it without alerting Nanette and Louis about what I was after. And my aunts..." He stared up at the ceiling.

"What is it?" My stomach tightened. Had he found something?

"Judith had been romantically involved with the man Anabelle shot, Perkin Moore."

"Yes," I said, "but we knew that."

"But Anabelle had been engaged to him first. They broke up, and he ended up with Judith."

I sucked in a breath. If Arsen and I broke up and he fell for Dixie, I'd like to think I'd be big about it and love them both. But I don't think I'd be able to pull that off. Not easily. "How did you find out?"

"I found the marriage license application for Anabelle and Perkin."

I pressed my hand to my stomach. They'd gotten as far as a marriage license? "Poor Anabelle." And yet the sisters had continued sharing a house. What must that have been like?

"It's the wedding dress and the fire alarm that bother me," he said. "It seems... unbalanced."

I sat up. The blanket slipped off my shoulder and puddled on the ebony cushion. "Yes, that's exactly it. I mean, anyone who commits murder has to have some level of...not necessarily insanity, but not rightness. Attacking the dress, pulling the fire alarm, those were malicious acts. And they were childish too. Spiteful. But I don't know any of our suspects well enough to have made them that angry at me."

"Except for my aunts."

"Who've never indicated a hint of derangement. And maybe the fire alarm had nothing to do with anything. Maybe it really was just some kid."

Arsen raised a brow. "You can't believe that."

"Of course I don't believe it. But we have to admit it's a possibility."

He rose. "All right. Playing devil's advocate isn't getting us anywhere. Let's get to that dinner."

The others were starting on dessert by the time we arrived on the restaurant patio. My mother paused, her fork poised above her tiramisu. "I hope your investigating was fruitful."

Beside her, my father shot her a warning look. She ignored it.

Arsen glanced at me. "You could say that." He pulled out a metal chair for me, and I sat, my face heating. Candles flickered on the tables. A warm breeze stirred the white tablecloths.

"Investigating?" Nanette shifted in her chair. Her expression tightened. "I suppose you had background checks run on us all?"

"Yes," Arsen said blandly.

Louis broke his slice of cherry pie with a fork. "Learn anything good?" the lawyer asked.

"Not really," Arsen said.

"How did Sophie usually spend her days when she was an *au pair*?" I asked, and everyone stopped to stare at me. "We've been talking about the day of the accident, but what was her routine?"

"Arsen would know that best," Louis said. "And I presume he can't remember."

"No," Arsen said.

"Did she ever bring Arsen to Angels Camp?" I asked Anabelle.

"Well, yes." Anabelle's full lips pursed. "She did. At least once a week. That nice young man of hers drove her. We'd play with Arsen. She and her boyfriend would go off on their own to wander the nearby woods. I think it was a nice break for them both. Arsen could be quite a handful even then."

"It couldn't have been quite as nice of a break in the winter," I said. I wasn't sure what I was digging for. But we still knew so little about Sophie. And *something* in her Doyle past had led to her murder.

"They had snowshoes," Judith said. "I remember admiring them so much I bought a pair for myself."

"Still," I said, "she must have felt a little trapped up at that big house." I nodded up the hill, where the mansion waited. "No one around, no shops within walking distance—at least not with a toddler." The more I thought about it, the less the idea of moving into the mansion appealed. Ever. Fortunately, we didn't *have* to move.

"I suppose so," Anabelle said vaguely. "We didn't really discuss it." A waitress in a tight black skirt and apron whisked past.

"We like the privacy that house provides," Judith said. "So did John and Bergdis."

"But they brought a stranger into the house," Arsen said. "An *au pair*. That must have been an adjustment."

"It must have been uncomfortable at first," Anabelle said. "It's always strange having an outsider living in your home. But they grew to love Sophie."

"And yet Bergdis accused her of theft," I said. "Stolen lingerie, I believe."

"Oh, that." Anabelle shook out her cloth napkin. "Bergdis wasn't herself. She was high strung."

"No." Judith's narrow face creased. "She wasn't. Not usually. Usually Bergdis was very level-headed. Grounded, they'd call her now."

"But she *was* high strung," Anabelle said. "Don't you remember when I'd gone upstairs to use the bathroom? I was having that embarrassing stomach complaint. When she saw me in the hallway, she nearly took my head off."

I risked a glance at Arsen. *Had* his mother been unbalanced?

"I remember you telling me that," Judith said, her expression impassive. "And I remember thinking how unlike her it was."

Anabelle sucked in her rosy cheeks. "You don't think I was making it up?"

"No," her sister said. "No, of course not. But the reason it was so hurtful to you was because it was so shocking. Losing her temper wasn't normal for Bergdis."

"You're right." Anabelle tapped her rounded chin. "And she apologized later. She told me..." Her brow puckered. "Actually, her apology was rather odd."

"Odd, how?" Arsen asked.

"Your mother was still obviously upset," Anabelle said, "though not at me. Bergdis told me she hadn't been sleeping. She said she felt like she was being watched. And—"

"Bergdis and John were under a lot of pressure at the time," Louis said, soothing.

The two sisters stiffened. "And I suppose that was our fault?" Anabelle asked.

"Of course not." Nanette sipped from her goblet of red wine. "It was a difficult time for everyone. The company was at a crossroads, and we weren't sure if we could or even should take that leap."

"Let's not talk about the past now." Louis raised his glass. "To the future, and to Susan and Arsen."

The others raised their glasses. "Here, here," my father said.

But a cold spiral writhed inside my stomach. The future. The past. The present. They were all entwined. And my instincts told me that a dark secret was threaded through them all.

Chapter 28

ON LADDERS, MY FATHER and Arsen hung twinkle lights high on the wall of the spacious barn. My mother unfurled a white tablecloth with a snap. It drifted atop a round table. She made a slight adjustment to the cloth.

Judith and Anabelle arranged the jade plants on a rustic ladder near the door. Nanette and Louis sat on sawhorses beside a long table and folded cloth napkins.

"I'm so pleased you're holding the reception here," Nanette said. "It brings back so many memories of John and Bergdis's wedding."

I nodded. We hadn't meant to hold our reception where Arsen's parents had gotten married. But there were limited options in Doyle.

I set down my ivy garland and frowned at a cluster of potted miniature trees. Dixie was supposed to be arranging them throughout the barn. Where had she gotten to?

My neck tightened. I understood that spending time with Ghost was difficult. But we were all adults, and there was a lot still to do before the wedding tomorrow. We were lucky the owner of the barn was letting us in tonight to prep everything.

I walked from the barn and looked around. The sky had begun to darken, an abalone sunset above the western mountains. At least Dixie's VW Bug was still in the dirt parking lot. She *had* to be around here somewhere. I strode toward her purple car.

A soft sob, almost a choking sound, emerged from behind a broad oak tree. My shoulders sagged, my heart pinching.

Dixie was crying? This had been harder on her than I'd thought. I should have taken it more seriously. I should have been worrying less about the wedding and more about my cousin. Well that ended now.

Feet dragging, I moved toward the oak. I'd been alone a long time before Arsen and I had become a couple. But the right man had come along. She'd find the right person too.

I walked around the tree. "Dixie?"

She gasped, and I stopped short. Dixie's back was pressed against the tree, Ghost's arms around her. What I could see of her clothing was in disarray.

Ghost looked over his shoulder and quickly stepped away. "Susan."

My face grew hot. "Ghost."

"Susan." Dixie scowled.

"Sorry," I babbled. "I was worried about you. I didn't know you, er... I'm glad to see you two are getting along again."

Arsen appeared at my side. "There you are." He took in the scene. Dixie's heaving chest. The color in Ghost's cheeks. He grasped my hand. "We've got to get back to Wits' End," he said.

"Right," I said. "Right. The gazebo."

He tugged me gently away. "Let's give these two some privacy," he said in a low voice. We walked toward his massive Jeep.

"Did you know—?" I whispered.

He laughed. "No. But it beats them snarling at each other over the wedding cake."

"The ivy wreaths are ready to be hung," I called back to the two. But I doubted they heard me.

Reluctantly, Arsen and I left the barn in the hands of our guests and returned to Wits' End. We carried cardboard boxes of ivy garland from the house and studied the gazebo.

A warm mountain breeze stirred the roses climbing the white-painted gazebo. The UFO fountain splashed.

"Does it really need more decoration?" Arsen asked. "I'm not being lazy here. I just think it looks great as is."

"People are used to seeing it as-is. This is a special occasion."

"The occasion's more than special." Shifting the box to one hand, he wrapped his free arm around my waist. Arsen pulled me in close, kissing my mouth. My heart beat faster. "And I'll do whatever you want to it," he said.

I almost told him to forget the schedule, we could string the ivy later. But once you start making excuses and going off-plan, a whole cascade of backsliding can result.

I swallowed. "I padded in some extra time to get this done. If we finish quickly, we could—"

"On it." He pulled an ivy vine from the box.

We anchored the vines on the hooks in the side of the gazebo. I'd added the hooks for just such an occasion. It was a popular wedding spot.

My parents arrived, and my mother swept out the gazebo. My father and Arsen unrolled a red carpet and arranged it inside the gazebo.

The bushes rustled on the nearby hillside, and I stiffened. Arsen rose swiftly. "Hello?"

My neighbor Sarah emerged from the manzanita bushes. She brushed a wisp of brown hair off her pale forehead. "Oh. Sorry. I was just looking for Fred."

"Fred?" Arsen asked.

"My Bantam rooster," she said. "I know he's probably gone for good, but I had some time on my hands and thought I'd... I know, it's silly."

"Not at all," my mother said. "It's a lovely night for a rooster hunt."

I shot her a sharp look. *Hunt?* That wording had seemed more than a little suspicious. Though in fairness, I wasn't exactly in mourning for the bird. Fred had been really irritating. I rubbed my watch.

"My husband's glad he's gone after what he did to his watch." Sarah hung her head. "He said he pitied the coyote that ate him."

"It's the circle of life," my mother agreed. "But we're sorry for your loss," she added insincerely.

"Are you going to replace him?" my father asked.

"No," Sarah said. "We never wanted a rooster, but you don't know what you're going to get until too late. The seller said we could return any roosters in the flock. But then they'd just kill them, and I couldn't do that to Fred. The kids had already named him. And he had gorgeous plumage."

"He was a fine looking fellow," my father said heartily. "Feathers so red they were nearly purple."

"That's exactly right," Sarah said. "I didn't realize you'd met him."

"We couldn't help noticing him perched on the fence," my mother said.

"He did love to find the highest perch." Sarah sighed. "Well, I'll leave you to it. The gazebo looks wonderful. We're all looking forward to the wedding tomorrow."

"So am I," I said.

We watched her slim form vanish around the corner of the Victorian. I glared at my parents. "I will not belabor the point. I've already told you how I feel about your behavior. But I'm still mad about it. Poor Sarah."

"What behavior?" My mother lifted her palms in a helpless gesture.

The phone rang in Arsen's pocket. He pulled it free, and his tanned brow wrinkled. He answered it. "Arsen here."

"Didn't you hear her?" my mother said. "She didn't want a rooster anyway. And I told you, we had nothing to do with it going missing."

Oh, *that* was believable. "Interesting wording."

"What's wrong with my wording?" my mother asked.

"You said you had nothing to do with it going missing," I said. "Maybe it isn't missing. Maybe you know exactly where its body is buried."

"Susan," my father said severely. "You know better than that. Why bother to bury it when there are scavengers about to dispose of the corpse?"

"I'll be right there." Arsen hung up, his jaw set. "I've got to go."

"What's wrong?" I asked.

"I've been called up, volunteer fire department." His hazel eyes had an agonized look.

"Oh, no," I said. Everything was so dry. Every fire had the potential to spread. "Where?"

He pocketed the phone. "The barn where we're having our reception," he said, grim.

Chapter 29

THE FIRE MIGHT HAVE *nothing to do with the murders*. My hands clenched on the wheel. Arsen's Jeep Commander sped before my SUV in the gathering gloom.

But what were the odds it didn't? The attacks were all alike. The destroyed dress, the pulled alarm at the spa... I should have known the mind of the killer would try something again.

Smoke darkened the tops of the pines as we bumped down the road toward the barn. A sheriff's deputy motioned for us to stop. We pulled off the road and leapt from our cars. The deputy nodded to Arsen as he raced past, recognizing him as a volunteer firefighter.

"Where's Sheriff McCourt?" I asked before the deputy could challenge me. "I need to see her."

He blinked. "She's at the fire."

"Good." I jogged after Arsen before the deputy could react. I rounded a bend.

Fire trucks surrounded the barn. Arsen joined the firefighters. Black smoke poured from its upper windows.

An ambulance stood nearby, its rear doors open. Two paramedics loaded a form on a stretcher through its back doors.

Judith studied the ambulance and looked grim. I hurried to her.

"Judith, what happened?" I asked. "Who...?"

"Anabelle." She swallowed.

I took an involuntary step backward, one hand pressed to my chest. "Is she going to be all right?"

"I don't know." Her mouth tightened. "One minute we were decorating. The next, smoke was billowing around us. We ran outside. I realized Anabelle wasn't with us." Her voice cracked. "Arsen's friend Ghost went back inside. He dragged her out."

A gust of acrid smoke stung my eyes, and I blinked rapidly. "And everyone else...?"

"They're fine. Everyone's fine. But Anabelle—" She covered her face with one hand.

I rubbed her back. The ambulance pulled away.

Judith made a sobbing sound. "I need to go with her."

"It's okay," I said. "My car's here. We'll follow them to the hospital."

The two of us hurried to my car. I drove Judith down the mountain highway to the hospital, a tall, blue-glass edifice outside of town.

After some chaos in the emergency room, a nurse led us back to a small room. Anabelle lay, her back raised on a cushioned table, an oxygen mask over her face.

Anabelle wrenched the mask from beneath her reddened eyes. Her face was streaked with soot. "She tried to kill me." Her voice slurred.

"We could have all been killed," Judith said. "That old barn was a death trap. I don't care if Bergdis and John held their reception there. We should have insisted on holding Arsen's reception at the house."

I stiffened, then forced my limbs to relax. It was ridiculous to get defensive about the barn now. Of course they were upset. And she was right, they all *could* have been killed.

"No." Anabelle wheezed groggily. "She hit me over the head. Bergdis tried to kill me."

Judith and I glanced at each other. *Bergdis?* "Where did this happen?" I asked.

"In the barn," Anabelle said.

"Where in the barn?" I clarified.

"I'd gone to the little girl's room. And when I came out, everything went dark. And then that handsome young man was carrying me like a sack of potatoes." Anabelle shook her head. Her twist of gray hair slipped loose, sliding down the pillow. "Like a sack of..." She rubbed her brow. "I never trusted Bergdis. John never should have married her. There were always too many men around her."

"Bergdis is dead," Judith said slowly.

"Of course she's not dead," Anabelle said. "How else could she have hit me?"

A doctor in a white coat walked into the exam room. "How are you feeling?" he asked her.

"My head hurts," Anabelle said.

"A headache is typical of smoke inhalation," the doctor said.

"Bergdis hit me," she said.

"The bruise on your head is likely from the fall, when you passed out," the doctor said. "Confusion after a fall isn't unusual," he told us. "Especially for someone her age."

"What's wrong with my age?" Anabelle asked.

"This seems *extremely* confused," I said. "She thinks her sister-in-law, who's been dead for decades, hit her."

"We'll keep her overnight," the doctor said. "She's got a concussion and smoke inhalation. Don't worry. We'll watch her."

"*I'll* watch her," Judith said. "I'm staying with her."

"Of course," the doctor said. "There's a bed for guests in the rooms. Someone should be here shortly to move her."

It wasn't shortly. It took thirty minutes for a nurse to wheel Anabelle from the emergency room. And then it took another thirty to get her settled in her room on the third floor.

The phone rang in my oversized purse. I dug it out. Arsen's name flashed on the screen.

"It's Arsen," I told Judith and answered. "Hi. I'm at the hospital with Judith and Anabelle. The doctors say Anabelle will be okay, but they're keeping her overnight. She's got a concussion and smoke inhalation."

He exhaled heavily. "I'm on my way to the hospital now. Everyone else is headed to Wits' End."

A machine by Anabelle's bed beeped. My chest tightened. "Why Wits' End?"

"I don't know. It's just what Nanette told me. You'd better get over there."

"I will. Arsen..." I trailed off, my heart turning to lead.

"I know," he said quietly. "I'll come to Wits' End later, and we'll... We need to talk."

I hung my head. "I know. I'll see you then. I love you."

"I love you too." He hung up.

"Don't worry about the reception," Judith said. "It may be short notice, but we can hold it at our house. I always thought it would be a better venue."

A lump hardened my throat. "Yes. We have options. Arsen's on his way here. I need to get to Wits' End. Apparently that's where everyone's gone."

"Go," Judith said. "We're fine here."

I nodded and hurried from the hospital, heat burning my eyes. We'd been fooling ourselves. How could the wedding go on after this? We should have called it off after Sophie's murder.

I drove to Wits' End. I sat in my car in the driveway. I stared at the Victorian's lit windows, at the moonlight glinting off the roof UFO. And when I thought I could speak to the others without crying, I walked inside.

Bailey met me in the foyer. I bent and stroked the beagle's soft fur. Then I followed the sound of voices into the kitchen.

"—a lawsuit," Nanette was saying as I walked through the swinging door. My parents, Louis, Dixie and Ghost fell silent. Nanette turned, and her expression smoothed. "How's Anabelle?"

"She has a concussion," I said. "They're keeping her overnight, but they think she'll be fine. What happened?"

Ghost grimaced. "I didn't see the fire start. One minute Dixie and I were, uh, outside. The next, people were racing from the barn and smoke was pouring from the roof. I found Anabelle near the bathrooms."

I nodded. "Anabelle said that's where she lost consciousness. Did anyone else see the fire start?"

The others shook their heads. "I was tying ribbons onto the backs of chairs," Louis said. "I didn't know what was happening until someone shouted."

"That was me shouting," Nanette said. "What do we do now? The barn's wrecked. There's no way we can hold the reception there tomorrow."

Everyone looked at me expectantly. I pulled my planner from my purse and set it on the kitchen table. I stared at the closed, leatherbound book.

There would be no answers inside. And even if there had been, I couldn't have used them. What came next was a decision Arsen and I would have to make together.

"I don't know," I said quietly. The question was no longer where we'd have the reception. It was *if* we'd have a reception, or even a wedding for that matter.

"The wedding's still on," Dixie said. "Right? I mean, that's happening here, at Wits' End."

"Arsen and I are getting married." One way or another, that would happen. "But I don't know if we can do it tomorrow. Arsen wants Anabelle there and... I don't know."

"All right," my mother said. "You and Arsen need to talk and make a decision. In the meantime, the reception in the barn is off. I'll tell the caterer to bring everything to Wits' End tomorrow. It's too late to cancel. We may as well get the food."

"Is the caterer even open at this hour?" Nanette asked.

"We'll find them," my mother said. "Hank?"

My father started. "Right. We'll take care of it. Don't worry. I'll get my keys." He strode from the kitchen.

"I suppose the photographer will also need to be informed," Nanette said. "Who else?"

"The band," Dixie said.

"Right," Nanette said. "We'll track them down."

"I've got their numbers," Dixie said. "Come on." She led Nanette into the parlor.

My mother hugged me. "We'll figure this out."

Numb, I nodded. I flipped through the wedding planner, searching for numbers to call.

An hour later, my parents were off hunting down the caterer. Dixie and Ghost had driven to a bar in Angels Camp to find the band, which was playing there that night. Nanette and Louis had returned to the mansion.

Bailey sat in my lap. He was a little too big to play lapdog. But I held him close, his warmth a comfort. The beagle seemed to know something was wrong. He snuggled close to me, his head on my chest.

The kitchen door swung open, and Arsen walked in. "Susan."

I set Bailey on the linoleum floor and rose. Arsen pulled me into a hug.

"How is she?" I asked.

"Confused. She kept insisting my mother knocked her out." He laughed hollowly. "Anabelle was very apologetic about it though."

"Everyone seems to assume the wedding reception is moving to Wits' End," I said. "I didn't have the heart to tell them there may not be a..." My throat closed.

He drew me outside. In silence, we walked down the porch steps and to the decorated gazebo. "We're getting married," he said firmly.

I nodded. But were we? Really?

He stopped at the gazebo steps. "But how much does this wedding matter to you?"

Water trickled in the UFO fountain. The scent of roses hung in the warm night air. Arsen's handsome face was serious, the full moon highlighting his chiseled features. And for the first time, the sight of that face made me want to cry.

I wanted to be with him so badly, forever. Was I being selfish? And suddenly I didn't care if I was. I didn't care about the wedding or the cake or the guests or the band. All I cared about was Arsen.

"The wedding doesn't matter at all," I choked out. "I just feel terrible that so many people are coming. But my parents are going to have the caterer bring the food here. So there'll at least be a massive picnic. And I'm not even sure we should do that. Not with..."

"Louis." Arsen's jaw hardened.

"It has to be him, doesn't it? He's back at the mansion now with Nanette. I almost said something to her when they left together. Should I have said something?"

"He has no reason to hurt her. And I called the sheriff on my way from the hospital. She's put a guard on Anabelle. She said she'd send someone to the mansion as well to let him know they're being watched."

I lowered my head. "I'm so sorry."

"If he was responsible for my parents—"

Something rustled in the manzanita bushes on the hillside. The moonlight illuminated a flash of scarlet plumage.

"Is that Sarah's rooster?" I asked.

"I'd better grab it before a coyote gets it." His grin was lopsided. "Or your parents." Arsen strode into the manzanita and cursed. "Get back here." He climbed further up the hill, vanishing beneath the pines.

I sank down on the gazebo steps. The sheriff wouldn't be able to arrest Louis before the wedding. There was no real evidence. Unless she had something I was unaware of. And the odds of that were low.

We'd have to call the wedding off. I didn't think I could stand to see his face, to pretend I didn't understand—

"There you are," Louis said, and I started.

He stared down at me and smiled.

Chapter 30

HE SHOULDN'T BE HERE. The thought must have shown in my face, because something in his expression shifted and grew cold.

"I thought you'd gone to the mansion with Nanette," I said, but my voice was a trifle too high. The moon slipped behind a cloud, darkening the yard. The silky ribbons on the gazebo grayed.

"There's a sheriff's car outside the mansion," Louis said blandly. "Do you know why?"

"With everything that's gone on, I expect they're trying to provide some extra protection."

He sat on the steps beside me. I shifted as if to make room, but the thought of him brushing against me raised the hair on my arms. *Arsen, where are you?*

"You really are like her, you know," he said.

Frost spread through my midsection. I knew the *her* he meant.

"Do you know why I'm here?" he continued.

And suddenly, I was sick of it all. Sick of the games. I'd pretended before, told myself I couldn't be sure. Because of my hesitation, Anabelle had nearly died.

I turned my head to face him. "I expect you've come to kill me, like you did Bergdis." My voice was steady, but I wanted to scream.

A low sound escaped his throat. "Yes."

We sat there for a long moment. My heart thumped so loudly I was sure he must have been able to hear the sound. The clouds parted, and the gazebo brightened.

"What happened?" I finally said. "Did Arsen's father catch you in the act?"

"Nearly. She was dead when he found her. He only had eyes for her—that never changed. He didn't see me in the shadows with the golf club."

"You killed him too. And then you put them both in his car, drove them to the cliff, and pushed the car off the highway." *Arsen. Be nearby. Be hearing this. Be ready.*

"Exactly as you say."

"You were obsessed with her," I said.

"I loved her."

"We don't kill the people we love."

He chuckled. "Nonsense. It happens all the time."

A chill wracked my bones. I gripped my elbows to keep from shuddering. Arsen had to be nearby. I hadn't heard any sound from him or the rooster. He *must* be creeping toward us, readying an attack.

"But Sophie saw something," I said. "Maybe she didn't understand it then, but it preyed on her mind. And when she returned for our wedding, she asked you about it. And you killed her."

"She saw me on the grounds that day, after she thought I'd left. Of course, I was at the mansion a lot longer than I said that afternoon, cleaning up. I didn't think anyone would come looking for evidence there. Not with the car accident happening on the highway. But I didn't want to be sloppy."

I felt the blood drain from my face. *Evidence.* There would have been blood splatters. *Blunt force trauma.* "Did you kill Sophie with the same golf club you killed Arsen's parents with?"

"I got rid of that club long ago. It belonged to Bergdis. No one missed it. I believe the club I used on Sophie belonged to Judith. Or maybe it was Anabelle." Louis shrugged. "Either worked."

Nausea twisted in my throat. "Junior saw you."

"He didn't see me kill anyone. He saw me throwing the golf club into the ravine. The poor fool couldn't resist attempting blackmail. I always suspected his resentment would be his downfall. He really thought the Holidays had cheated his father." He clucked his tongue.

"The pulled fire alarm, the dress... I thought it was a warning to me, to stop investigating. But it was all about Bergdis, wasn't it?"

He was the one who'd stolen her lingerie all those years ago. He'd been there that day, acting as Sophie's advocate, or at least pretending to.

"I saw that dress, the dress *she'd* worn, and... You shouldn't have taken it. It didn't belong to you." His voice shook. "It was hers and hers alone. You were stepping into her shoes, or you were trying to. But you're only a pale shadow of what Bergdis was. The young are so arrogant these days."

He was insane. How had he functioned so long as a corporate lawyer with no one noticing? How had he hidden it so well?

"And then patronizing that spa," he continued. "The spa she'd helped start. Like you were the new lady of the manor. It was sickening."

"And using the barn where she'd held her reception? Was that why you set it on fire?" Beneath me, the gazebo steps were hard and cold.

He frowned. "It really was where they married? I thought Nanette was confused. All those old barns look alike. No, that fire was to cover up Anabelle. She'd seen me in town when that fire alarm was pulled. Of course, she couldn't believe it. She had to talk to me herself, didn't want to falsely accuse an old friend. Silly, stupid woman. No one saw me slip after her into the hallway, wait for her to come out of the ladies' room. I set the fire and returned to my post tying those damned ribbons on chairs. Who comes up with these idiot decorating ideas? By the time the fire got going, I'd knotted three more ribbons. I didn't think Arsen's friend would play the hero and save her."

"She's under guard now," I said.

"I know that. Why do you think I'm here? By tomorrow, she'll have her brain back in working order. She'll put it together. She'll know my excuse for being in Doyle doesn't hold water. She'll blab. Anabelle never could help herself. She nearly got her sister put away all those years ago because of it."

The air left my lungs as if I'd been punched. "Are you saying Judith murdered that man?"

He gave an elegant shrug. "Who knows? He followed her back to her place, looking for a fight. But Judith had a temper. She'd egged him on. It was his choice to break into their house, but she pushed him to it. And Anabelle was the one who shot him."

He pulled a slim, black gun from the pocket of his blazer and pointed it at my temple.

The moon hung low over Wits' End. I could see the rabbit, a gray silhouette dancing across its bonelike surface. On the gabled roofline, the edge of the UFO glinted, as cold as the glint of the gun.

"Is that Judith's?" I croaked.

"Yes. I didn't think to bring my own on this trip. Well. Goodbye, Susan."

"Drop it," a hard, masculine voice said from behind us.

I started. I almost hadn't recognized the voice as Arsen's, it was so filled with rage.

"Ah, Arsen," Louis said. "Why don't you come around to the front of the gazebo?"

"Drop the gun," Arsen repeated, emerging from the shadows.

"Why?" Louis asked. "You're not armed."

"I said—"

"Do you want to watch me shoot her?" Louis asked.

"Not to be trite, but you know you can't get away with this." Arsen's voice was an angry growl. "Anabelle will talk to the sheriff. The others will put it together."

"I know," Louis said. "There's no point to pretending anymore."

"My mother figured you out," Arsen said. "She knew you'd long stopped being her faithful knight."

A faint squawk emerged from the bushes.

"I was always her knight," Louis said bitterly. "But she never saw it. She never saw past your father," he spat.

"And he never saw you for who you were," Arsen said. "Maybe he didn't want to see it. But you've always been good at hiding your true nature. You fooled me."

"You were easy." Louis's upper lip curled. "So trusting. So needy. So desperate for a father figure."

Arsen's neck corded. His hands were tight fists.

"No," I said. "He isn't any of that. You only ever saw what you wanted to see, Louis. You saw Bergdis loving you, and she didn't. You saw me usurping her place, and I never tried, never could."

The lawyer smiled faintly. "Love is blind." A faint scratching came from behind the UFO fountain, trickling loudly.

"No," I said. "That's not true either. Love sees people for who they are and loves them anyway, because love is bigger than our imperfections."

"If Bergdis had shared your philosophy," Louis said, "things might have been different." He aimed his gun at Arsen. The cuff of his jacket slid up his wrist. Moonlight glinted off his gold watch. Arsen's shoulder muscles bunched.

SQUAWK! A blur of red exploded from behind the fountain. Louis pivoted, aiming.

Arsen launched himself at the lawyer. The gun went off. I screamed.

The two men crashed into the fountain, the bird flapping and squawking around their heads. The fountain tipped, water splashing onto the lawn. The UFO spun whitely across the grass.

Louis grunted and went limp. Arsen rose above him, his hand clenching the gun. Blood streamed down his temple.

"Arsen," I whispered. Shakily, I clambered to my feet. "You've been... You're hurt."

He swiped his hand across his face and glanced at the blood on it. "I'm fine. I cracked my head on the damned fountain. Call the sheriff."

I fumbled my phone from my pocket. The bantam fluttered to the gazebo railing. A gold watch dangled from its beak.

"Arsen—"

"It's over," he said. "Finally."

Chapter 31

"So he killed all those people over a woman?" In my bedroom, Dixie stepped back and frowned at the mirror. She wore an Army-green silk dress that skimmed her shoulders. Outside, music played faintly.

I turned in the glass. The dress was simple, a long white strapless. I could have worn it anywhere. It wasn't special. There were hundreds out there like it. But it was special to me now, and I smoothed its silky front.

"It was that horrible, age-old story," I said. "Louis couldn't have her, so no one could. Unfortunately, Arsen's father arrived too late to save her and too late to realize what was happening."

My throat caught, remembering the look on Arsen's face last night, when he thought *he'd* been too late. I coughed. "But Arsen's father could connect Louis to the murder, so he had to die."

"And Sophie saw him."

"She saw Louis at the mansion after he should have left, or after he'd seemed to have left. And he never mentioned it to the police. Of course, Sophie didn't know that at the time. But the deaths of Arsen's parents stayed with her. She couldn't stop thinking of them. She'd even collected newspaper articles about the investigation. No one mentioned Louis being at the mansion later. So when she came to Doyle for the wedding, she asked him about it."

"And he killed her."

"And once again, someone saw something they shouldn't have."

"Junior," she said, "who was dumb enough to try to blackmail a triple murderer."

I plucked my bouquet of Gran's roses from the dresser and sighed. "We all like to think we're smarter than a killer. But he wasn't. Junior thought this was finally his chance to get the money he thought he was owed."

"At least Anabelle was able to make the wedding," Dixie said. "Why'd she think Arsen's mom hit her back at the barn?"

Anabelle had admitted to me this morning she'd felt insecure around Bergdis. Anabelle hadn't seen who'd hit her, but her jumbled brain had made her old rival the villain. "She was just confused."

Dixie pulled a piece of paper from her pocket and unfolded it.

"Is that your prayer?" I asked.

"No, it's the stupid to-do list you gave me. It says I'm supposed to encourage you and calm your nerves. Are you calm?"

I looked down at my hands, holding the bouquet. They weren't even a little damp. And the shadow of anxiety that had haunted me for years... wasn't there. "I'm good."

"Need encouragement?"

"Not really." It was all I could do not to go flying out of the B&B and rush the wedding.

"Need me to talk you out of this? It's not too late to punk out, you know."

"I'm not punking out. And speaking of which, why *exactly* did Ghost ditch your Vegas meet-up?"

"A friend of his got assaulted and wound up in the hospital. His mother called and begged Ghost to help track the creep down. I guess she thought he might come after her son in the hospital. Ghost caught him inside the hospital disguised as an orderly, waiting to make his move."

"Whoa," I said.

"I know. It's all a little too high drama to be believable. But the news picked it up, so it's been verified. Of course, Ghost could have planted the story, but my sources say it was legit."

My gaze clouded. "Ah, ha." *Planted? Sources?* Dixie really *hadn't* been taking any chances.

She shrugged one shoulder. "I guess I can't bust his chops over it. It was sort of life and death. And I did make it hard for him to apologize afterward."

"How?"

"I changed my name on all the UFO chatrooms so he couldn't find me. Not the ones that switched to calling themselves UAP chatrooms though. They're dead to me. That's why he broke into my trailer. He thought I was the same person, but he wasn't sure until he got onto my laptop. That guy can hack," she said admiringly.

Outside, the music changed. My stomach fluttered, and I took a deep breath, swallowed. "I think that's your cue."

"Gotcha. See you on the other side." She walked from my bedroom.

I followed more slowly into the kitchen. My father rose from his chair. "Susan. You look beautiful."

I kissed his cheek, then peeked out the window above the sink. Guests fanned themselves in folding chairs on the Wits' End lawn. The morning was getting warmer, and my heart warmed with it. In spite of all the wedding chaos, nearly everyone was there.

The sheriff and her plus one, Enrique. The Bonheim sisters and their husbands and boyfriends. Sal and Bingo from Nowhere. Nanette and Judith and Anabelle. And others too—Antoine from the western bar, and three old men holding garden gnomes, and my neighbor Sarah and her squirming family.

A flash of scarlet winked from a post in the white picket fence. The bantam menace threw back his head and crowed.

And Arsen, waiting at the gazebo with Ghost at his side and Bailey at his feet. My eyes heated, and I blinked rapidly.

Arsen.

A breeze fluttered the gazebo's climbing roses. The rooster hopped from his perch and strutted across the lawn. I hoped everyone had been warned to hide their watches.

Maybe there was no perfect ending. Maybe there was no happily-ever-after either. But Arsen was waiting for me, and I'd take that today.

My father offered me his arm, and we stepped onto the porch. The guests in their chairs turned toward us. A smile spread across Arsen's face. And we walked down the porch steps.

Note from Kirsten:

I LOVE A HAPPY ending. And writing this book put me in a very good mood, so I hope you enjoyed reading it. But Arsen and Susan's adventures aren't over. Next up—a honeymoon in Sicily! Like honeymoons, this story will also be short. Expect *Revenge of the Ziti* in late 2023...

It's been an idyllic Italian honeymoon for lovebirds Susan and Arsen, as they explore the winding streets of romantic Sicily. Even better for B&B-owner Susan, she's enjoying staying in someone *else's* bed and breakfast, even if that someone else is a tightly wound innkeeper who reminds her a little too much of herself.

But sunny Sicily takes a dark turn when the newlyweds discover a body on the inn's private grounds. In this locked-garden mystery, any of the quirky guests could be the killer. With danger lurking around every corner, Susan and Arsen must navigate newlywed bliss, Sicily's historic hilltop towns, *and* the twists and turns of murder. But will they be able to uncover the truth before the killer strikes again?

If you love quirky heroines, twisty mysteries, and laugh-out-loud humor, you'll love this short mystery, book nine in the Wits' End cozy mystery novels. Buy *Revenge of the Ziti!*

More Kirsten Weiss

THE PERFECTLY PROPER PARANORMAL Museum Mysteries

When highflying Maddie Kosloski is railroaded into managing her small-town's paranormal museum, she tells herself it's only temporary... until a corpse in the museum embroils her in murders past and present.

If you love quirky characters and cats with attitude, you'll love this laugh-out-loud cozy mystery series with a light paranormal twist. It's perfect for fans of Jana DeLeon, Laura Childs, and Juliet Blackwell. Start with book 1, *The Perfectly Proper Paranormal Museum*, and experience these charming wine-country whodunits today.

The Tea & Tarot Cozy Mysteries

Welcome to Beanblossom's Tea and Tarot, where each and every cozy mystery brews up hilarious trouble.

Abigail Beanblossom's dream of owning a tearoom is about to come true. She's got the lease, the start-up funds, and the recipes. But Abigail's out of a tearoom and into hot water when her realtor turns out to be a conman... and then turns up dead.

Take a whimsical journey with Abigail and her partner Hyperion through the seaside town of San Borromeo (patron saint of heartburn sufferers). And be sure to check out the easy tearoom recipes in the back of each book! Start the adventure with book 1, *Steeped in Murder.*

The Wits' End Cozy Mysteries

Cozy mysteries that are out of this world...

Running the best little UFO-themed B&B in the Sierras takes organization, breakfasting chops, and a talent for turning up trouble.

The truth is out there... Way out there in these hilarious whodunits. Start the series and beam up book 1, *At Wits' End,* today!

Pie Town Cozy Mysteries

When Val followed her fiancé to coastal San Nicholas, she had ambitions of starting a new life and a pie shop. One broken engagement later, at least her dream of opening a pie shop has come true.... Until one of her regulars keels over at the counter.

Welcome to Pie Town, where Val and pie-crust specialist Charlene are baking up hilarious trouble. Start this laugh-out-loud cozy mystery series with book 1, *The Quiche and the Dead.*

A Big Murder Mystery Series

Small Town. Big Murder.

The number one secret to my success as a bodyguard? Staying under the radar. But when a wildly public disaster blew up my career and reputation, it turned my perfect, solitary life upside down.

I thought my tiny hometown of Nowhere would be the ideal out-of-the-way refuge to wait out the media storm.

It wasn't.

My little brother had moved into a treehouse. The obscure mountain town had decided to attract tourists with the world's largest collection of big things... Yes, Nowhere now has the world's largest pizza cutter. And lawn flamingo. And ball of yarn...

And then I stumbled over a dead body.

All the evidence points to my brother being the bad guy. I may have been out of his life for a while—okay, five years—but I know he's no killer. Can I clear my brother before he becomes Nowhere's next Big Fatality?

A fast-paced and funny cozy mystery series, start with Big Shot.

The Doyle Witch Mysteries

In a mountain town where magic lies hidden in its foundations and forests, three witchy sisters must master their powers and shatter a curse before it destroys them and the home they love.

This thrilling witch mystery series is perfect for fans of Annabel Chase, Adele Abbot, and Amanda Lee. If you love stories rich with packed with magic, mystery, and murder, you'll love the Witches of Doyle. Follow the magic with the Doyle Witch trilogy, starting with book 1, *Bound*.

The Riga Hayworth Paranormal Mysteries

Her gargoyle's got an attitude.

Her magic's on the blink.

Alchemy might be the cure... if Riga can survive long enough to puzzle out its mysteries.

All Riga wants is to solve her own personal mystery—how to rebuild her magical life. But her new talent for unearthing murder keeps getting in the way...

If you're looking for a magical page-turner with a complicated, 40-something heroine, read the paranormal mystery series that fans of Patricia Briggs and Ilona Andrews call AMAZING! Start your next adventure with book 1, *The Alchemical Detective*.

Sensibility Grey Steampunk Suspense

California Territory, 1848.

Steam-powered technology is still in its infancy.

Gold has been discovered, emptying the village of San Francisco of its male population.

And newly arrived immigrant, Englishwoman Sensibility Grey, is alone.

The territory may hold more dangers than Sensibility can manage. Pursued by government agents and a secret society, Sensibility must decipher her father's clockwork secrets, before time runs out.

If you love over-the-top characters, twisty mysteries, and complicated heroines, you'll love the Sensibility Grey series of steampunk suspense. Start this steampunk adventure with book 1, *Steam and Sensibility.*

Get Kirsten's Mobile App

Keep up with the latest book news, and get free short stories, scone recipes and more by downloading Kirsten's mobile app. Just click HERE to get started or use the QR code below. Or make sure you're on Kirsten's email list to get your free copy of the Tea & Tarot mystery, *Fortune Favors the Grave.* You can do that here: KirstenWeiss.com or use the QR code below:

Connect with Kirsten

You can download my free app here:
https://kirstenweissbooks.beezer.com
Or sign up for my newsletter and get a special digital prize pack for joining, including an exclusive Tea & Tarot novella, *Fortune Favors the Grave.*
https://kirstenweiss.com
Or maybe you'd like to chat with other whimsical mystery fans? Come join Kirsten's reader page on Facebook:
https://www.facebook.com/kirsten.weiss
Or... sign up for my read and review team on Booksprout:
https://booksprout.co/author/8142/kirsten-weiss

About the Author

I WRITE LAUGH-OUT-LOUD, PAGE-TURNING mysteries for people who want to escape with real, complex, and flawed but likable characters. If there's magic in the story, it must work consistently within the world's rules and be based in history or the reality of current magical practices.

I'm best known for my cozy mystery and witch mystery novels, though I've written some steampunk mystery as well. So if you like funny, action-packed mysteries with complicated heroines, just turn the page...

Learn more, grab my **free app**, or sign up for my **newsletter** for exclusive stories and book updates. I also have a read-and-review tea via **Booksprout** and is looking for honest and thoughtful reviews! If you're interested, download the **Booksprout app**, follow me on Booksprout, and opt-in for email notifications.

BB bookbub.com/profile/kirsten-weiss

g goodreads.com/author/show/5346143.Kirsten_Weiss

f facebook.com/kirsten.weiss

instagram.com/kirstenweissauthor/

Made in United States
North Haven, CT
15 June 2023

37809038R00127